Exiled

by

L. Rosario

Exiled

COPYRIGHT © 2007 by L. Rosario

Contact Information: info@thewildrosepress.com

Cover Art by *RJMorris and L. Rosario*

The Wild Rose Press
PO Box 708
Adams Basin, NY 14410-0706
Visit us at www.thewildrosepress.com

Publishing History
First Scarlet Edition, 2007
Print ISBN 1-60154-175-9

Published in the United States of America

Nadia dragged her attention back to the man's eyes, dying to know what color they were, and held her ground as he approached. No one in their right mind would forgo the chance to sink their teeth into such a divine treat, and if he turned out to taste like the ocean, she'd chew some gum afterward.

He halted, leaving a few feet between them, but it was close enough for her to see that his eyes were some nondescript hazel color. It was the sort of color that changed depending on what the person had on, and she wondered what color they would be if he were naked. The dark baggy shorts and loose, white tank top did not necessarily showcase the body underneath, but they could not hide the defined muscles of his shoulders. No one could have shoulders like that without having the rest of the package to match.

"Are you out here alone?" Mmm. His voice carried just a hint of an unexpected accent. Although too subtle to place, it stirred memories of Jason murmuring to her in his native Portuguese, which was odd considering this man couldn't look more California surfer if he tried.

His question seemed an odd way to start a conversation, but it was better than her asking him to bare his neck. "I am, yes."

His gaze swept the beach before coming back to her. "Should you be?"

"A few moments ago, I might have answered no, but now I'm beginning to think coming here was an excellent idea."

Dedication

As always, a huge thank you to my wonderful editor and loving family.

Reviews

5 out of 5 Angels for L. Rosario's first book,
Captive Fantasy
available online at Amazon

"...Captive Fantasy is by far the most engaging and erotic story I have ever read...funny, romantic and hot! This is a story that is going to make your blood boil. L. Rosario is definitely a must read author for [readers of] both erotic and paranormal romances. She is one author I will not be able to get enough of."
Amanda—Fallen Angel Reviews

Chapter One

Villa Sangue—Coven house, Santa Fe

Nadia slammed into her bedroom with enough force to rattle the candles in their sticks and shake the pictures on the wall. Jason, one of her three human servants, lounged on the bed where she had left him just moments ago. At the time, he'd been naked and resting after a vigorous bout of lovemaking. Now, he wore sweats and had a book open in his lap. Nice of him to get comfortable while her world crumbled around her.

He looked up, and whatever he saw on her face made his swarthy, olive complexion actually go pale. "What happened?"

The words stuck in her throat. If she said them out loud she might cry, and she wouldn't do that, not even in front of Jason. She stomped to the bed, tore the book from his hands and threw it to the floor. Her actions only deepened the concern on his face.

Ignoring the look, she gestured toward his sweats. "Take them off." Sex would make her feel better. Sex and blood. Never had the combination failed to undo the wrongs life thrust upon her.

Jason obeyed, still regarding her with open concern but wisely holding his tongue. Once naked, he stretched onto his back and waited as she stripped out of her dangling, platinum belt and black, tunic sweater.

The outfit had been chosen with the utmost care, in response to the master's summons, but what good had it done her to wear what she knew he liked? Not once had he even glanced at the exposed length of her pale legs or the vibrant spill of her red hair against the black fabric. She could have answered the summons naked for all he seemed to care.

A fresh wave of pain threatened to consume Nadia, but she shook it off and crawled on top of Jason, melting into the warmth of his skin. He was always so warm, so mortal.

"Nadia," he began, but she cupped her hand over his mouth. She didn't want to listen to his questions or feel forced to offer answers. He'd learn soon enough what had happened.

He kissed her palm, and the concern deepened in his dark, brown eyes. It was moments like this when she was awfully grateful he could not read her thoughts, but that didn't mean his probing gaze wasn't uncomfortable. There were other ways to read a person than getting into their mind, after all, and Jason always seemed in tune to her feelings and moods. Though a blind man would likely be able to read the pain in her features if even half of what she felt shown through.

She looked away, partly to hide her expression but mostly to avoid such a look of loving concern. She did not want Jason's love right now. She wanted an obedient servant. Someone bound by blood to give her everything she demanded. Someone to take away the sting of being told...no, she would not relive the awful words.

Focusing on the dark stubble lining Jason's jaw, Nadia moved her hand just enough to feel the rough texture under her palm. Jason always looked best when he was a bit rough around the edges. It lent him an air miles apart from the polished perfection of her master.

Good Lord, as if the two men could ever fairly be compared. One was a kid off the streets, while the other, well, there were not words to do him justice.

"Nadia." Jason had escaped her hand, and his voice ended the unsafe path of her thoughts.

She met his gaze and shook her head. "No. Not a word, do you understand? I don't want to hear a single word from you."

He nodded, but his expression was far from obedient. "Just one question, and then you'll have my silence."

Nadia rolled her eyes. Jason never did take orders well, so why on earth did she keep him around? Oh yeah, he tasted delicious and he fucked like an animal.

3

"One question," she agreed. He smiled, drawing her gaze to his sexy mouth. Yet another reason he was still in her bed. Lips that made a woman come just by looking at them were hard to find as well.

"You've been exiled, haven't you?"

Nadia forgot all about Jason's mouth. She pushed away to sit up, and he let her go, not even reaching for her as she left the bed. She crossed her arms, not to hide her nakedness, but to let him know he'd asked the one question he really shouldn't have.

"Why do you say that?" Even she wasn't fooled by the tight tone of her voice.

Jason rose up on his elbows and tossed his shaggy, black hair out of his eyes. "So, I'm right."

Saying yes would make it all real. Turning away, Nadia plucked her sweater off the floor and began to fight with the sleeves in order to pull it over her head. The bed moaned, and Jason grabbed her from behind, settling his hands at her hips. His touch warmed her from head to toe, but it did nothing to the chill deep inside.

"You can't be surprised," he said.

Nadia threw the sweater back down and turned within Jason's hands. She cupped his face and forced his head back so she could see under his unruly hair and into his eyes. "Yes, believe it or not, I am surprised. And would you like to know what surprises me more? That you seemed to expect this. Care to tell me why?"

Jason shrugged. "Chase and I have been expecting this ever since the master took a queen."

Nadia's temper ratcheted up a few degrees. "You and Chase are not here to speculate on such things. You are here to provide me with blood." She fell silent for a moment. "Why didn't you mention Lukas? Didn't he expect this as well?"

"Lukas is too distracted by himself to care what happens to you." If it weren't true, the flippant reply would have infuriated her. She'd chosen poorly when it came to Lukas, not that it mattered anymore.

"Before you get all freaked out," Jason went on, "Chase and I don't spend the bulk of our time expecting bad things to happen to you."

"How lovely to know that," Nadia purred.

Jason trapped her hands against his cheeks. "Everyone inside this house has been waiting for the queen to point her finger at you, Nadia. You have to have realized that?"

She did, but was that supposed to make her feel better right now? Did it somehow change the fact that she had to leave? No.

Pulling away from Jason, she crawled back onto the bed. "I don't want to talk anymore." She patted the mattress, and like a good servant, Jason stretched out and tucked her against his side. His heart pounded in her ear, and she moved closer to let the rhythm soothe her.

"Tell me what I can do for you," he offered.

If only he could really give her what she needed, but no one could undo what had happened in the master's study. The past, no matter how distasteful, could not be altered. Believing sex and blood could cure this was nothing but a fantasy, but what else could she cling to when the reality hurt so damn much?

Placing her hand over Jason's heart, she stared at the contrast of her white fingers against his darker skin. He only had a few black hairs sprinkled across his chest, despite the heavy stubble on his jaw and the crisp hair covering his legs. Maybe age would bring more, but now she'd never know.

Oh God...

"Nadia?"

She shook her head, unable to speak. Tears threatened, but she blinked them back and concentrated on the skin close to her mouth. She slid her cheek along his chest and kissed the side of his nipple. It puckered in response, begging to be captured between her teeth. Needing a powerful distraction, she clamped her mouth around the tight bud and pierced the skin with her fangs.

Jason threaded his hands into her hair and held her close as she drank, but she didn't feast for long. Releasing his nipple, she soothed the wound with a few laps of her tongue then licked up the side of his neck. He arched, moaning softly, and wrapped his arms around her to pull her fully on top of him. She buried her face in the crook of his neck as his hair fell away, smelling everything she craved; blood, flesh and sex.

His fingers flexed at her waist, and he shifted her over his groin, letting the hard, persistent head of his cock part the curls between her legs. He was as ready to give as she was to take.

Nadia latched onto Jason's neck and slid her sex along the length of his erection. He swallowed, making the skin between her teeth pulse and tear. She tasted blood just as he slipped inside, and she circled her hips to force him deeper. Normally, she'd take him slow, one glorious inch at a time, but not now. She wanted it all and slammed her pelvis against his to let him know it.

Jason bucked off the bed and plunged his hands into her hair again. With a strong pull, he moved her away from his neck, smiling at her irritated growl. Before she could shake free and get back to what she wanted, he pressed her face close and captured her mouth in a searing kiss. The lips she adored mastered hers for several moments before his tongue thrust past them to fuck her mouth. Down below, his cock moved in perfect tandem.

Caught up in the intoxicating rhythm, Nadia nearly missed the sound of the door opening and closing. Footsteps padded toward the bed, and every nerve ending went on alert seconds before a hand brushed up her spine. She shivered, and Jason moaned.

"Mind if I join in?" The quiet question caressed with the same gentleness as the hand running up and down her back.

Jason ended the kiss and met her gaze with a look of raw anticipation. "I don't mind if you don't mind." As if he really needed to ask.

Nadia tossed a look over her shoulder to see her other servant patiently awaiting an answer. Where Jason was all smoldering, dark, sex appeal, Chase was angelically beautiful. At times, he seemed too lovely to be real and much too precious to handle life as a vampire's servant. He held her gaze and stepped out of his loosely tied, gray lounge pants. Naked, his angelic beauty took on an oddly naughty appeal.

Nadia lowered her gaze, past the toned torso and flawless skin to zero in on the rampant evidence of his desire for her. The sight tightened her muscles around Jason's cock, forcing a sharp intake of breath from him, but she kept her attention on Chase. After several moments, she returned her focus to his face and nodded.

Grinning, he wasted no time crawling onto the bed and positioning himself behind her. He straddled Jason's outstretched legs and took hold of her hips. Nadia pushed back until the tip of his erection teased the crease between her buttocks. His fingers flexed, and he nudged forward.

"May I, mistress?"

Ah, Chase, always the gentleman. Even with his cock poised to claim her ass, he begged permission. Out of the three of her servants, he was the only one able to take her like this. Jason and Lukas were just too damn big, but Chase was long and slender. Perfect.

Nadia buried her face in Jason's neck, lifted her hips higher and breathed the word, yes. Clearly eager, Chase pushed forward, spread her with just the tip of his cock then stopped. A little wiggle of her hips forced him deeper, but far from deep enough. The teasing promise of having his slender length fully imbedded almost made her whimper. To avoid letting the pathetic sound escape, she licked the side of Jason's throat until his blood rose to the surface to warm the skin.

Oh God, what was Chase waiting for? Before she could lift her head to demand he finish what he started, he pushed forward again but then withdrew.

"You aren't quite ready yet, mistress."

Not ready? Was he crazy? She was so wet it soaked her thighs—the thought ended as Chase pressed his face right where his cock had been. Nadia stifled a groan against Jason's neck as fresh juice oozed down the sides of his cock. And to think, she'd thought herself wet before.

Chase licked her with focused determination, making her throb around the hard thickness of Jason's cock. Jason moaned softly and began to thrust into her, increasing the torment of Chase's tongue whether he intended to or not. It felt so damn good, and yet, she feared she might die before either of them did enough to make her come.

"Boys, please." She mumbled the words against Jason's neck, and Chase's smile tickled her ass. She should have known all he wanted was to make her beg for it. Angelically beautiful or not, Chase could be an imp from time to time.

Kissing a path from her ass to the small of her back, Chase shoved inside again. This time, there was no resistance, and he buried himself to the hilt just as Jason reared up under her. Nadia gasped, biting hard into Jason's neck.

Chase's thrusts burned as he fought against the tight confines of her passage, bringing the sensation awfully close to discomfort, but she loved every moment of it, and he knew it. His grip tightened on her hips to slam her ass against his pelvis as he thrust again. Jason picked up the rhythm with ease, and she gulped his blood while they fucked her in tandem.

In tune to her needs, Jason rolled his head to the side to allow her full range of his neck while Chase held onto her hips and pounded into her like a jackhammer. It was hard to say which one of them managed to hit the happy spot first, and it didn't really matter. All that mattered was the lovely feel of Jason's skin tearing under her fangs and the hot gush of blood into her mouth just as her body exploded around both their cocks. Each pulse brought on another wave of pleasure, and the orgasm went on and on until she feared it would never end.

It would serve her master right if she died of pleasure and denied him the satisfaction of watching her walk away. The thought should have brought a smile to her face, but it only served to dim some of the ecstasy of the moment. Damn that man.

Thankfully, Chase trailed his hands up her sides then around to cup her breasts, squeezing and tugging her nipples to the point of pain. As a distraction, it worked wonders, allowing her to focus on the warm weight of his body as he curled over her back. Thoughts of the master vanished under the weight of Chase's body pinning her against Jason. Hot breath puffed along her nape as Chase's thrusts reached a frenzied tempo, and with a rumbling growl, he came in an explosion of hot semen.

Nadia ceased to feed, content to simply hold Jason's skin between her teeth and enjoy the feel of Chase emptying himself deep inside her. After a final shudder, and a sigh she'd never forget the sound of, he withdrew and flopped onto the bed beside Jason. She looked over, but his arm was slung across his face, hiding his eyes. His chest rose and fell as if he'd just run a marathon, and the pale hairs dusting his pecs looked black thanks to a fine sheen of sweat. The urge to reach for him was strong, but she kept her hands safely buried in the pillow above Jason's shoulders.

Chase peeked out from under his arm, and his lips split into a lazy grin that made her gut clench. His mouth might not pack the punch Jason's did, but it was still nice.

Nadia couldn't help but smile back, though the joy she felt was short lived when Chase dropped his arm to fully expose his eyes. Like the rest of him, they were almost too beautiful to be real. Once a person recovered from the shock of such a rich shade of blue, there was the intensity of his stare to contend with. At times, it even stole her breath.

God, she'd miss looking into those eyes. She'd miss watching them fill with emotion, with love for—

"Hey, my turn." Jason tugged on her hair to regain her attention. "You haven't forgotten about me, have you?" He punctuated the question with a wicked roll of his hips. As if she could forget the thick cock wedged deep inside her.

Not willing to speak around the emotions threatening to undo her, Nadia captured Jason's mouth and let him suck the flavor of his blood from the tip of her tongue. Groaning, he clasped her with his teeth and held tight while increasing the tempo of his thrusts. Her breasts brushed his chest as he rocked her, making her cry out each time her nipples touched flesh.

The cries became shrieks of pleasure once

Chase wedged his hand between them to pinch her nipple. He chuckled, and his turquoise eyes sparkled when she met his gaze. "If it's too much, I'll stop."

Nadia shook her head. These boys did not know the meaning of too much, nor would she get the chance to teach them. Anguish threatened to ruin an otherwise delightful moment, so she stared into Chase's eyes and ground her hips hard against Jason. "I'll let you know if and when it becomes too much."

"Yeah, okay, you do that." Chase rolled to his side, propped his head in his hand and continued to torment her nipple while Jason tried to buck his hips.

"Jesus, Nadia, are you going to let me come or not?" His face was set in a mask of determination when she met his gaze. "It's not fair to let Chase finish and make me suffer."

"Awe, poor baby" She pushed her breast into Chase's palm and lifted her hips to free half of Jason's cock. Immediately, he took hold of her waist and held her right where he wanted her so he could drive into her over and over again.

Once, twice, three times was all it took until his semen shot into her with vengeance. The force of his release caused a mini orgasm of her own. Gasping, she squeezed her eyes shut and enjoyed the moment.

"Dammit, you've made me hard again," Chase said into the heavy silence that followed.

Nadia dropped her head to Jason's shoulder

to smother the sound of her laughter. She shouldn't have anything to laugh about, dammit. She'd been exiled from the coven and told to vacate before sunrise. And yet, here she was, fucking her two favorite mortals as if she had not a care in the world. Was she crazy?

Lifting her face from the sweet smell of Jason's sweaty skin, she glanced toward Chase who now lay with both hands propped under his cheek. He looked just like an angel with his big blue eyes, platinum hair and smooth skin, and the affection in his eyes brought an unwelcome burning behind her lids. Would he miss her as much as she would him?

The thought undid all the pleasure sex had brought.

With a curse, Nadia got off Jason, who did nothing to stop her. She could feel two sets of eyes boring into her as she left the bed and reached for her sweater. Jason knew enough not to speak, but Chase...

"What's wrong, Nadia?"

She yanked her sweater on to stall for time. At least Jason had guessed, preventing her from having to say the horrible words out loud. Chase, however, was an eternal optimist, and there was no way he'd assume she'd been exiled, regardless of how much speculating he and Jason might have done.

"Nadia?" The concern in Chase's voice stabbed at her heart.

"You can tell him, Jason." Kicking her fallen

belt out of the way, she stalked to the mirror to finger-comb her hair. Within the cloud of blood-red waves, she looked paler than usual, and pinching her cheeks and licking her lips offered little improvement. For the first time in one hundred years, she looked like what she was, a walking corpse.

In the reflection, she watched Jason shift his attention to Chase. "She's been exiled."

Chase's gaze widened and flew toward the mirror. Nadia had to close her eyes against the anguish on his face.

"When do you have to leave?" God, was his voice shaking? She'd never be able to handle it if he actually cried over losing her. "Nadia?"

She opened her eyes and met his gaze in the mirror. Damn, the turquoise was definitely brighter than usual. "Don't you dare cry for me, Chase."

He sat up and avoided the hand Jason tried to wrap around his arm. "When do you have to leave?" he asked again.

Nadia swallowed a combination of regret, longing and the lingering taste of Jason's blood. Not a good mixture. She slid her gaze from Chase's and stared into her own eyes. The slate-blue had a sheen to it she'd rather not contemplate. No tears, dammit.

"I've been given until sunrise, but I think it best to leave now."

The bed protested as Chase launched himself across the room. He reached her in four strides and grabbed her arm to spin her around. His rough handling caused her hair to slither over her shoulders and land like a bloody blanket across his hands and forearms.

Nadia stared at the spill of hair, and her throat constricted. How many times had Chase laughed while she trailed her hair over his—

"I'll leave with you. It doesn't matter where you decide to go."

Oh God. Nadia met Jason's sad gaze over Chase's shoulder. She couldn't do this. Why must the master force her to do this?

Chase shook her lightly. "Look at me," he demanded. She did. "Tell me I can come with you." A single tear hovered on his lower lashes.

Nadia was too much of a coward to speak, but she managed to shake her head. While Chase stared at her in wounded shock, Jason sucked in a loud breath. The master had told her she must leave alone, and for that, she'd never forgive him. Didn't he realize what it felt like to leave behind parts of your soul?

Unable to tolerate the heavy silence or the accusation on the faces she'd never see again, she ripped free of Chase's grip and ran for the door. It slammed behind her, but it couldn't block the sound of Chase's choked sobs or Jason's angry curses. With a curse of her own, she collapsed against the door and sank to the floor in a miserable heap, burying her face against her knees to hide the tears. When had she turned into such a coward?

A change in the air let her know she was no longer alone, and she didn't need to lift her head to recognize the crackling aura. Only one person was capable of sending hot sparks over her skin without even touching her. Very slowly, she looked up.

The master stood at the top of the stairs with the entire length of the hallway separating them, and yet he might as well have been lying naked on top of her. Yes, what she felt for him was that strong.

"Are you ready to go?" The sound of his voice was pure torture, as was the lack of emotion in his eyes as they moved over her face.

Would it kill him to care just a little bit about her? She latched onto the budding anger and ran with it. "Have you actually come to say good-bye?" All the pain she felt poured into her scathing tone.

It seemed the master might smile, but then he shook his head and stepped closer. Every inch of her flesh tightened with annoying awareness. Why hadn't she realized from the beginning this man could never be hers? Maybe later she'd admit she'd brought this exile on herself. Maybe.

"Nadia, you've left me no choice. Surely you understand?" He shoved his hands in the pockets of his black pants and continued to stroll toward her. The black jacket he'd worn earlier, while telling her the news, was gone, leaving his white dress shirt fully exposed. The sleeves were rolled to his elbows, and the collar gaped to the center of his chest. On him, casual looked naughty.

She tore her gaze from the smooth skin peeking out from his shirt and regretted it the moment she met his eyes. Transfixed, she could only stare as he rifled through her thoughts. Whatever he found caused a frown to tug at his lips. Releasing her from his gaze, he sighed, and the sound caressed her like a warm hand.

"I cannot allow you to take your servants. I am sorry you have been forced to say good-bye."

His words were shocking enough to dull the sexual awareness inside her. "Did you just apologize to me?"

He nodded and completed his route to her. Halting before her, he studied every feature on her face and extended his hand. She didn't want to touch him, and yet, it was the only thing she wanted to do. Sliding her hand into his, she held his gaze and stood.

"Had she not come into my life..." He shrugged.

For the second time that evening, Nadia was damn close to hysterical tears. "Saying that does neither of us any good," she bit out. "All it does is make me hate her more." Not for the first time, she pictured her master's precious queen and wondered what the hell that woman had that she lacked. The woman had been mortal, for God's sake. Powerful vampire masters did not take mere mortals and turn them into queens.

Too fast to comprehend, his hands were around her upper arms. His rough touch forced her tears closer to the surface. "She is my soul, Nadia. I won't apologize for that. Ever."

Nadia swallowed a sob and focused on the master's mouth. It had to be safer than his eyes. Or not. She licked her lips and thought of all the things she'd never been able to do with this man, and all the things she longed for, even now. Perhaps he'd grant her one kiss? A memory to take along.

He released her and stepped back before she could form the question. "I've asked Fabian to see that you are somewhere safe by sunrise."

So much for that kiss.

Nadia gave a single nod and hugged herself. "What will become of my servants?" The thought of her boys bound to other vampires tore at her already wounded heart, but she knew from having lived within the coven for so long, how things worked. Jason, Chase and Lukas would be given a choice, and if they chose to stay, they would need new masters.

"Nadia, you know the way of things. I'll be as fair as I can be with them and honor whatever choices they make."

She nodded but found it impossible to speak.

The master cupped her chin to lift her gaze. "I'll give them my blood to sever your bond. It will dull the pain of separation."

"For them." But what of her pain?

"Would you have me take your memories before you go? Ask, and I'll do so."

Oh God, he'd send her away with nothing? Quickly, she shook her head and freed her chin from his grasp. "No, I'll be fine. Do what is necessary for them, that is all I ask, and make sure their new masters are kind."

"I do not allow cruelty here, Nadia, nor would the queen tolerate it." The mere mention of the woman sliced fresh pain through Nadia.

"Fine." Her tone was curt and bordering on disrespectful, but she didn't care. She needed to get away...from here, from him...before she did something she'd regret for the rest of eternity. Something stupid, like dropping to her knees to beg for a morsel of his affection to take with her.

Focusing on the stairs and the soft drone of voices drifting up from the gathering room, she wondered if her exile was the talk of the evening. How long would she be whispered about? And worse, would she be used as some sort of coven example? At least no one would know if she failed to survive on her own. The exile might kill her, but the coven would never know.

The thought brought her gaze back to the master. "Will you care if this kills me?"

His expression went blank. For too long, he merely stared at her with cold, dead eyes until her skin began to crawl and she regretted asking the stupid question.

Nadia finally looked away, unable to take

another second. "Forget I asked." She took a step away, but he caught her hand and stopped her. She stared at his fingers around her wrist. Tears threatened again.

"You are too strong to let this exile kill you," he told her. "You and I both know that."

Nadia licked her lips while memorizing the way his long, pale fingers looked against her flesh. A woman needed something to dream about, after all. "I don't wish to leave," she said quietly.

"Then swear fealty to Sylvia and take your rightful place in this coven." He made it sound so simple.

She jerked her gaze to his face. "I can't." He released her, and there might have been a flash of sadness in his gaze. It was there and gone much too fast for her to be certain.

"Yes, I know. And for that reason, you must go." Shoving his hands into his pockets, he backed toward the stairs. "Fabian will bring a car around. I suggest you pack and leave without any further delay." With that, he turned and left her.

Nadia fisted her hands at her sides and cursed every vampire in this coven. Maybe she'd find someone on the outside desperate for some vampire kills? Maybe she'd make them a map and give them her key? Maybe—

Her thoughts came to a screeching halt, and she felt the master's hand reach inside her mind. He might not be present, but his power still lingered.

You'll do no such thing.

Nadia ground her teeth together.

Nadia. Even in her thoughts, his voice evoked undeniable power.

"All right," she snapped out loud. "I'll do no such thing." His power began to recede, leaving her feeling cold and rejected. Wow, this really sucked.

"What was that all about?" Jason's voice scattered whatever remained of the master's hold on her. He stepped into the hall, carefully shutting the door behind him.

Dressed in snug black jeans that time had turned nearly gray and an untucked black T-shirt with a chipped Harley Davidson logo on the front, he looked good enough to eat, and yet she only wanted to weep. His black hair gleamed from the quick shower he'd probably taken, and he smelled strongly of musk. Whatever he'd splashed on to cause the crotch-tightening scent wasn't aftershave because his jawline was still covered in stubble.

"Well? Gonna tell me why you were talking to yourself just now?" He flashed a cocky grin and raked his fingers through his hair.

Nadia ignored the question. "Is Chase all right?"

"No." Jason was never one to mince words. "But he'll survive."

"You'll watch over him, right?" My God, would this horrible nightmare ever end? Her throat burned, her eyes burned, hell, everything burned, and she had yet to utter the word good-bye.

Jason nodded. "Yeah, of course. Where will you go?"

"I don't know." Shrugging, she hugged herself and stared at Jason's bare feet. "Fabian is to make sure I'm somewhere safe by dawn."

"Hey?"

She didn't want to, but she looked up into his eyes. The affection staring back at her did her in and tears started streaming down her face. Jason growled softly and pulled her into a tight embrace. Burying his face in her hair, he stroked her back and promised everything was going to be okay.

It was a beautiful lie.

Chapter Two

Nadia slouched in the backseat of the fancy Hummer and glared out the window. She could barely see anything since the tinting was so dark, but the view was better than the back of Fabian's head.

"Pouting won't change anything, you know?"

"Do not talk to me." Nadia kept her attention on the window, but she could feel Fabian looking at her. Shouldn't he keep his focus on the road?

"I'm surprised it took the queen this long to have you removed."

"Okay, obviously you are not going to shut up." She slid her gaze toward the front seat and clashed with Fabian's green eyes in the rearview mirror. She'd never really liked him, but she despised him at the moment. "Do you think I care what you or anyone else in that God forsaken coven thinks?"

He laughed and shifted his attention to the road. "Curious where I was told to take you?" he asked after a while.

"No." But she was, and unfortunately Fabian was powerful enough to pluck the truth right from her thoughts.

"I was told not to tell you." Laughing, he shot her a look in the mirror. "And some of us actually follow the master's rules."

"Well, I hope you win the lap dog of the year award then."

He laughed harder. "Tell me you regret it, at least."

"Why? So you can report back to him?" Nadia shook her head. "No, if that is what you are fishing for, forget it. I refuse to apologize for my feelings."

"Women always fall in love with the wrong guy."

"I'm sorry, Fabian. Were you hoping I would fall for you?" He had a better chance of sprouting wings, and they both knew it.

"At least if you had, you wouldn't be on your way out of town."

Nadia shrugged and returned her gaze to the window. "I don't want to talk anymore so leave me alone and drive."

"Are you worried which one of us will claim your servants?"

"You are beyond annoying, Fabian."

"Not everyone thinks so." He winked when she glanced at him. "So, are you worried? If not, you should be because I know who wants the pretty one."

"His name is Chase." Nadia ground her teeth against the urge to demand a name. It did not matter though. Chase was no longer her responsibility, and she knew Jason would look after him.

"You're dying to ask, I can see it on your face even without hearing it in that head of yours. Pepper."

The name was like a hot slap across the face, and Nadia gasped. "Tell me you're lying."

Fabian shook his head, a triumphant grin spreading across his rugged face. "It's true. She was telling all of us at the gathering last night that he'd be hers the as soon as you were gone." He glanced at his watch. "I'd say he's hers by now."

Seeing red, Nadia bit her tongue hard enough to draw blood. Pepper had been sniffing around Chase ever since he'd become Nadia's. Damn her. It wasn't a case of being afraid Pepper would harm Chase, it was just the simple fact of having lost something to the raven-haired bitch. Pepper would strut around for weeks, gloating.

"Hey, you won't be there to see it, so chill."

"How is that you are over five hundred years old and yet you talk like a sixteen year old mortal?"

"I have evolved." Fabian grinned again. "Evolution insures survival."

"Oh, spare me the great wisdom of our master." Fabian's laugh filled the spacious vehicle, making Nadia wish she could simply open the door and leap out. "Wherever you are taking me, be quiet until we get there, okay?"

His eyes twinkled in the mirror. "If I agree to that, do I get rewarded?"

"Sure." She'd agree to anything to get him to shut up. Ah, where was hindsight when you most needed it?

True to his word, Fabian was silent for the rest of the trip, which took hours. Finally, they reached wherever it was they were, and he parked, turned off the Hummer and twisted in his seat to look at her.

"Proud of me?"

Nadia rubbed her eyes and glanced out the window. "Where are we?"

"Sorry, can't tell you that either."

Scowling, she took in the long, narrow motel they were parked in front of. "Are you dropping me off here?" The thought of what the rooms might look like behind those matching red doors terrified her.

"It's clean, I promise." Fabian hopped out and appeared at her door to open it and reach in for her. She resisted, but he simply took her hand and pulled her out. "Be good, Nadia, or I'll be forced to get ugly."

"Do you really think you are all that handsome now?" Actually, he wasn't bad with his bright green eyes and close-cropped black hair, but she'd never admit that out loud.

He leaned close to her, eyes twinkling. "We both know you've secretly wanted me for years."

"And if I admit to that will you tell me where I am?" She dropped her voice and fiddled with the collar of his shirt. As always, he had the first five buttons undone to show off his well toned chest, and she slipped her fingers inside to brush against his smooth skin.

"I might tell you where you are if you do more than admit you want me."

She lifted her gaze to his. "Which room is mine?"

His eyes widened. "Damn, I can't read your thoughts right now. Are you kidding me?"

She moved her hand down his body to find the rock hard erection in his pants. "Can you only focus on one thing at a time? Poor Fabian." He pushed against her hand, and his lids drooped. "I had no idea how badly you wanted me. How cruel of me to make you suffer all this time."

"God, Nadia," he snarled. Digging his hands in her hair, he jerked her head back and aimed for her mouth. "Now that you're out of there, I can finally have a taste."

She jerked her head to the side at the last moment, and he kissed her jaw with a low growl.

"You say that as if the master would have punished you." She pushed against his chest as he continued to seek out her mouth. "Fabian, stop it."

He straightened and glared at her. "You fucking tease." His grip turned brutal in her hair, and there was no chance of overpowering him as he once more yanked her head back.

Instead of aiming for her mouth, he went for her throat and scraped his fangs along her skin.

Nadia braced herself for the bite but still winced when Fabian's teeth pierced her. He sucked hard, taking more blood than anyone had a right to. She struggled, unmindful of the way his teeth ripped at her skin in response, and managed to escape his teeth. He growled and pinned her against the car before she could complete her escape.

"Not so fast, you little whore."

"I am not a whore." Nadia clawed at his scalp, wishing he had hair long enough to grip, and still he drank. "Fabian, don't do this." If he took too much blood, she'd crave it to the point of being a danger to the first mortal she saw. Not that there seemed to be any in this desolate place.

Finally, he lifted his head and smacked his lips together. "If I thought I could get away with it, I'd keep you hidden somewhere." He palmed her breast and squeezed with the same brutality he'd used to restrain her. "I bet you'd be one hell of a fuck."

"Too bad the master disagrees with you." She pushed, and he backed up. "Now that you've had a snack, tell me which room is mine so I can get away from your vulgar company."

But he wasn't through with her, it seemed. Once again, he pinned her against the car. "Did the two of you ever..." He arched a brow.

"Why do you even think that is your

business?" As if she'd admit out loud that she'd never had the one thing she wanted more than anything.

"Ha! The master is a bloody fool."

"You are very lucky he isn't here to hear you say that, and I suggest you wipe that thought clean before you return."

"Do you think he'll exile me as well? I could come back for you, and we could live happily forever after." He waggled his brows and leered at her. "Sound good?" His cock dug into her as he pushed forward. "Just think how much fun we could have."

"If that happens, I'll schedule a date with the sun at high noon."

"Such uncalled for drama." Shaking his head, he released her. "Your room is number twenty-five, at the end over there." He pointed. "I hope you find the accommodations not to your liking."

"Ha ha." Nadia brushed by him and headed toward her new home. God help her. "Be a good lap dog and get my bags."

The inside of room twenty-five actually surpassed her expectations in that it had a large, clean looking bed and a full length mirror opposite. There was also a chest of drawers with a TV on top and a small bathroom, which was also clean. It could be worse, much worse.

Fabian dropped her bags just inside the door. "Last chance to sample what tons of ladies have squealed over." He held his arms out and nodded. "You know you want to."

Nadia slammed the door in his face. Fabian's arrogant chuckle penetrated the barrier and faded as he walked away. Alone at last, she turned to the room and sighed. A hot shower always made her feel better, so that would be her first order of business. Plucking a nicely folded towel from the foot of the bed, she headed for the bathroom, trying not to think about what the master had said to her, but it was too late. Talk about a memory that would haunt her forever.

She is my soul...

As if a vampire needed a soul. Ha! And it wasn't the actual words that haunted but the look that had been in his eyes when saying them. God, the intensity had been breathtaking. Never before had so much emotion filled those blue eyes. Never.

Sylvia didn't deserve to be the recipient of such emotion. For Pete's sake, the woman was nothing. A mortal the master had found God knows where and only a short time ago. Had they even known one another long enough to be one another's souls? Never mind that the bitch had willingly sacrificed her mortality to be the queen of the coven. What did that matter when Nadia would give whatever she possessed as well?

It just was not fair, and maybe if she kept mulling over the situation she'd eventually hate the master? At least hate would give her the strength to prove to him she could not only survive exile, but thrive in the midst of it. And that was exactly what she planned to do. Thrive.

Realizing she'd forgotten her robe, Nadia left the shower on to heat and returned to the bedroom. Halfway across the room, reality decided to rear its hideous head, and she stumbled a little and collapsed on the bed with the towel in her lap. Oh God...she was in exile.

Suddenly the room, although pleasant, was nothing but a prison. The silence screamed at her until her ears rang, and she covered them to block it out. Emotions swelled, a lump formed in her throat and her eyes began to burn. No, she would not cry. She would not...the tears started one by one, and then the dam burst.

Shaking and terrified to admit that she was not only alone but lonely, Nadia fell back onto the bed, buried her face in the towel and gave in to the raw emotion ripping her apart. At the moment, it sure as hell did not feel as though she'd survive even her first night away from the coven. Where was she going to find blood or sex or anything? She didn't even know where she was, thanks to that bastard, Fabian, following the rules.

The tears continued to fall, and her sobbing echoed around the room. Never had she felt this helpless. "Damn you, Master!"

Screaming the words changed nothing.

Exiled

Chapter Three

Nadia scowled as a wave swept over her toes then rolled back into the ocean. Moonlight flickered over the black water, and all around her, was a sense of calm. It should have been a beautiful moment, but she hated the beach. The pungent smell of fish clung to the inside of her nose, and the salty air made her skin tingle. She had no idea why she was even out here, but it seemed like a good place to think, and that was the one thing she really needed to do.

After spending the first twenty-four hours of her exile in hellish shock, holed up in that cheap motel room with towels draped over the windows and the television blasting to drown out the sound of her sobbing, she refused to spend another moment wallowing in self pity.

In time, the tears had dried, and she'd gathered enough peace of mind to remember she was a century old vampire. Not all vampires survived that long, and damn if she was willing to let her existence end now.

Rummaging through the chest of drawers had revealed a map and her location. Obviously the master hadn't even wished to keep her in

New Mexico because Fabian had driven her all the way to California. The discovery had brought on a flash of brilliance, and she'd left the beige prison, booked the last seat on a bus due to depart late at night and headed north to San Francisco, which just happened to be where Seraphina lived.

To Nadia's knowledge, Sera was the only vampire to ever voluntarily leave a coven. Who better to run to? Surely Sera would sympathize with her and point the way to some safe, fresh blood.

The thought made Nadia's fangs stir. Obviously, she hadn't had a drink since leaving the coven, and Fabian's little nip at her neck did not help matters. The longer she went without, the weaker and more vulnerable she would become, not to mention desperate. She'd give anything to have the taste of Jason or Chase on her tongue, but thinking about them would only bring back the pity and the tears.

"You have to get yourself together, girl." Her voice could barely be heard above the sound of the ocean, but it felt good to speak out loud, and it gave her the strength to square her shoulders and get on with things.

First on the agenda was a trip to Captive Fantasy to find out if the owner, Valentino, would take her to Sera. Considering what he and Sera had gone through to be together, one would think they'd still have a relationship. Only one way to find out.

Nadia gave the ocean one last look before stepping back out of the surf. Maybe the first thing she needed was a shower to wash away the stench of the beach. Yes, excellent idea. She turned from the water's edge, intent on making a quick detour back to her motel room, but took only one step before stopping to stare.

A man strolled toward her with his head down and his hands shoved into the front pockets of his long shorts. He had the kind of stride that screamed familiarity with the stubborn sand, and even in the moonlight she picked out sun-bleached strands snaking their way through his otherwise caramel-colored hair. If she needed further proof of his affinity for the beach, it was there in the golden hue of the skin left bare by his tank top.

Looking him up and down, she realized the only thing missing was a surfboard. Ick, he probably tasted like the ocean, and she wasn't that hungry. Before she could escape without notice, his head came up and their gazes met. He stopped, and Nadia continued to stare.

The highlighted hair feathered over his forehead, nearly eclipsing his eyes but doing nothing to hide the raw masculinity of his features. His strong nose might have dominated his face if not for the lush mouth below and the perfect line of his jaw. Lips quirking, he started toward her again.

Nadia dragged her attention back to his eyes, dying to know what color they were, and held her ground as he approached. No one in their right mind would forgo the chance to sink their teeth into such a divine treat, and if he turned out to taste like the ocean, she'd chew some gum afterward.

He halted, leaving a few feet between them, but it was close enough for her to see that his eyes were some nondescript hazel color. It was the sort of color that changed depending on what the person had on, and she wondered what color they would be if he were naked.

The dark baggy shorts and loose, white tank top did not necessarily showcase the body underneath, but they could not hide the defined muscles of his shoulders. No one could have shoulders like that without having the rest of the package to match.

"Are you out here alone?" Mmm. His voice carried just a hint of an unexpected accent. Although too subtle to place, it stirred memories of Jason murmuring to her in his native Portuguese, which was odd, considering this man couldn't look more California surfer if he tried.

His question seemed an odd way to start a conversation, but it was better than her asking him to bare his neck. "I am, yes."

His gaze swept the beach before coming back to her. "Should you be?"

"A few moments ago, I might have answered no, but now I'm beginning to think coming here was an excellent idea." Her meaning wasn't lost on him, and he flashed a heart stopping smile that revealed perfect white teeth.

"Before I get my hopes up, tell me why you're alone on the beach, at midnight." He took a few more steps toward her, and she caught the fragrance of his skin. Coconut. Now why wasn't she surprised?

"I came here to think." Nadia glanced toward the ocean and watched while a wave washed over the shore. The air stirred beside her, and when she turned, she looked right into a pair of mischievous hazel eyes, which at the moment held more green than any other color. Standing this close, not only could she smell his skin, she could hear his heart racing. He didn't know enough to fear her, so she assumed it was excitement.

"What does a pretty thing like you have to think about so deeply that you need this sort of solitude?" He swept his arm out to encompass the vast beach. To her surprise, instead of shoving his hand back into his pocket, he lightly brushed a few strands of hair back from her forehead. Their skin didn't touch, but the air between them thickened into something palpable and rare enough not to ignore.

Nadia took the final step that separated them and felt the heat pouring off his body. Her mouth watered with the need to feed, and she wanted to rip the tank top off him and rake her nails over his chest while burying her mouth against his throat.

Despite how lovely his face was, it had not escaped her notice that he possessed a neck any vampire would kill to bite. Thick cords ran up either side of his throat, and his pulse visibly beat at the base. The sight called to her already enflamed hunger, and she stifled the urge to lunge at him.

"Believe it or not," she forced out, around her lengthening fangs. "I have a great deal to think about." Very lightly, she trailed her fingertips up his left arm, making the muscles dance and tighten in the wake of her touch. "But I've done all the thinking I want to do for one night." She lifted her gaze to his and caught the hunger there. "I want you."

He took a step back as if she'd struck him, and laughed nervously. "You don't waste time, do you?" Still facing her, he continued to move away.

"Is there a point to doing so?" Nadia dropped her shoes and followed his backward progress through the sand. Now that she knew what the night had in store, she was very eager to get on with it. First some blood then she'd see if the naughty glint in this man's eyes matched his sexual prowess. She certainly hoped so.

He retreated and she stalked, until the soft sand gave way to sharp gravel and his back connected with the wooden surround housing a rather primitive looking shower head. His eyes widened when she didn't break stride but lost much of their unease the moment her body melted against his.

He gripped her shoulders briefly then slid his hands deep into her hair to yank her face back. "What exactly are you after?"

Nadia lowered her gaze to his mouth, then further still to his neck. She licked her lips and let the hunger seep into her voice. "I'm after you and everything you have to offer." She expected him to say something or ask more questions, but he did neither. Wrenching her head back again to see her eyes, he smiled and captured her mouth.

He did not taste like the ocean after all. Oh no, he was much more delicious than that. She sipped the minty flavor from his tongue as he shoved it into her mouth. The taste, along with the coconut smell of his skin, made her liken him to a decadent after-dinner treat. Yes, it had been a very long time since anything resembling food had melted in her mouth, but she could still recall the joy of savoring a good dessert, and this man brought all those memories back.

Originally, she'd been unable to think of anything but getting her fangs into his veins, but now she wanted to lay him out on the sand and nip at him from head to toe. Or maybe she'd start at his feet and work up? And maybe she'd lick him instead. At first anyway, then she'd sink her teeth into him, perhaps starting with the hard muscles of his shoulder, which currently flexed under her hand.

A groan built at the back of her throat but

never had the chance to form as the kiss deepened. Any noise she might have made, he immediately took into his mouth and swallowed before thrusting his tongue over hers again. The depth and ferocity of the kiss staggered her, and she had to clutch at his shoulders to keep her spine from bowing. She couldn't recall the last time her knees had been weak, but they barely supported her now.

Clearly, she'd been without blood for too long. What other possible explanation was there?

Finally, he pulled back, keeping his mouth just above hers. He opened his eyes, but only enough to peer at her through long, dark lashes. "Wow."

Nadia smiled at first, but then gave into the swell of laughter racing up her throat. It burst out and echoed around the deserted beach. Horrified, she slapped a hand over her mouth and ducked her head to hide from the amusement on his face, but his grip on her hair easily forced her gaze back up.

"Sorry." He smiled around the apology and shrugged one shoulder. "I didn't think any other word really applied."

Nadia shook her head and finally lowered her hand. "No, don't apologize." She brushed her index finger over his lips. They were still warm from the kiss and a deeper pink than before. "You're mouth is stunning."

It was his turn to laugh, though he did so

with a bit less gusto. "Thank you, but yours isn't too bad either."

She knew how beautiful she was, but still she smiled at the compliment. "Before you came along, I was heading back to my motel to take a shower. To be honest, I despise the smell of the beach, and I can't imagine taking this little encounter further until I've washed it away."

"That's an easy fix." He released her and positioned her a few steps back, until she stood on the sand once more. Grinning, he reached behind his back, and in a matter of seconds a narrow stream of water gushed out of the shower head. "I think this will do just fine, don't you?"

She opened her mouth to answer but held her tongue as he stepped away from the spray of water to take his tank top off. Muscles stretched under his skin as he flung the shirt far from where they stood. She'd barely registered the full glory of his torso before he reached for his shorts. They were so baggy, once he undid the first button they simply fell to his feet, leaving him clad in the smallest bathing suit she'd ever seen on a man. At least she thought the scrap of white was a bathing suit. Whatever it was, she liked it. A lot.

Despite the minuscule size of the swimsuit and the impressive package within, she dropped her gaze to his thighs as he backed up again. Muscles danced under his skin then tightened as the first drops of water hit. Following the stream of water upward, she watched as it cascaded between his pecs, down his tight abdomen and past the suit to finally reach his legs. It was as if the water taunted her, silently provoking her to let her mouth follow the path it took. The sight, the thought, all of it made her knees weak.

With a quiet but tortured groan, Nadia quickly took off her clothes. The priceless silk blouse deserved better than being tossed onto the sand, but she didn't care. Her jeans were next, followed by her bra and panties. Naked, she stepped forward, too impatient to allow him any time to gawk and enjoy the view.

Flattening her hands to his warm chest, she moved him aside just enough to let the water splash over her. It was cold but felt surprisingly good as it streamed down the line of her spine. "Mmm."

"It's pretty cold, isn't it?"

Nadia shifted slightly so she could lift her head without getting water in her eyes. "It's actually freezing, but I like it. Very invigorating."

He chuckled and took hold of her shoulders to plant her back against the rough wooden wall. The water fell unchecked between them but then bounced off his shoulders as he moved toward her. Pinned by his body, she felt the trapped line of his erection and suddenly hated the sinfully tiny bathing suit. She wanted him naked.

Lowering her hands, she slid her fingers into the waistband and brushed against the hidden drawstring. She coiled the cord around her first two fingers and pulled it free, using it to ease the suit away from his body. With her other hand, she pushed at his chest until he took the hint and stepped back. Water ran down the center of his body to disappear into his suit.

His stomach muscles contracted as he sucked in a shocked gulp of air. "Fuck, that's cold."

Nadia used the drawstring to pull him forward again and clucked her tongue. "Such language in front of a lady. Shame on you."

"Forgive me for saying this, but you don't look or kiss like a fucking lady."

His intentional cursing made her smile. She'd always liked the spice of rebellion in her men. It made their blood taste oh so yummy, and the taking of it a great deal of fun. "Lucky for you, right?"

"Yeah." He bent down to brush his lips across hers. "I feel pretty lucky right now."

Hopefully he'd feel the same tomorrow when he woke up with vague memories and a little bit less blood.

****

Daniel Rebiero had been looking for some time alone when heading for the beach. He liked to clear his mind and loosen his muscles with a little yoga before going to work, and the sound of the waves and the smell of the ocean always brought a sense of peace. The one thing he hadn't been looking for was an insanely sexy and mysterious redhead who seemed horny enough to fuck him senseless. But hey, if life offered, who was he to say no?

"You gotta name, gorgeous?" He kissed her lush lips again while pressing his body into her naked curves. His skin was hot, despite the cold water cascading over them, but she felt like pliable marble. God, he'd feel really bad if this little encounter left her sick. Maybe it'd be better to take her back up the beach and into the warmth of his bed?

She plunged a cold hand down the front of his swimsuit, ending any thought of going anywhere. Daniel hissed and pressed into the tight grip of her icy fingers.

"Do names really matter?" Her voice was a silky purr close to his ear then her lips slid down his neck, followed by the spine tingling stroke of her tongue. All the while, her fingers flexed around his cock, trying to stroke but unable to do so thanks to the tight fabric of his suit.

Fuck, he needed to be naked. Now. But that meant having her let go, and well, maybe naked could wait.

"I doubt you'll remember me come morning, so why worry about knowing my name?"

Jesus Christ, was she nuts? How the hell could he possibly not remember this in the morning? Hell, he couldn't wait to get to the club later tonight and tell the guys about the sexy beach goddess he'd managed to land. If he did land her, that is. She might just freeze his dick off first.

"Fine, no names." Daniel reached down to encircle her narrow wrist. His fingers went all the way around and then some, and the delicate pressure of her bones against his palm made him feel like a brute.

He wasn't a big guy, by any means, but he had enough muscle to be impressive and worry he might hurt her. If he'd ever had a woman who felt so fragile in his arms, he couldn't recall. Most of his lays were leggy, busty armfuls with loads of sun-bleached blonde hair and easy smiles. This sleek redhead was like a stolen sample of the finest caviar, and he was sort of afraid someone would toss him out of the party before he actually got to try some.

If ever there was a reason to stop thinking and start acting...

Meeting the woman's gaze and marveling at the odd pewter color of her eyes, Daniel held her arms at her sides and took a step back to disconnect his body from hers. "With or without your name, I promise to remember you come morning." That made her smile, or partially smile. Her ruby lips quirked at one side, showing just a small glimpse of white teeth.

"We'll see, won't we?" Her gaze swept downward, burning through his suit as if she had her hand on him again. "Do all men wear such interestingly tiny swimsuits in San Francisco, or are you an exception?"

He couldn't help but laugh. If she thought his swim trunks were tiny what would she think of what he worked in? "I might be an exception, but I don't come to the beach to look at the other guys." He shrugged and stifled the rest of his laughter as her gaze met his again. "I do know that the women favor small suits."

"And I'm sure you love them for it." Her tone was practical, not jealous.

"Sure, why wouldn't I? But to be honest," he hesitated and tilted her face up. "I prefer what you're wearing." Before she could do more than quirk her lips again, he kissed her. Like before, he was baffled by the fact that she didn't taste like anything. There was no lingering flavor of mint toothpaste or wine or anything. Everyone tasted like something, but she didn't. Hell, did it really matter?

He kissed her long and deep, forcing her to open her mouth wide to accommodate the rough thrusts of his tongue. While he explored the unique cavern of her mouth, she worked a hand inside his suit again. He was ready for the chill this time and managed not to hiss when her fingers curled around him. With the other hand, she pulled his suit away from his body, allowing her the freedom she needed to stroke his dick from base to tip.

Jesus Christ.

Kissing became an impossible thing to

concentrate on when her fingers crept lower to cup his balls. With a mixed sound of pleasure, shock and ecstasy, Daniel gave up on her mouth and simply buried his face against her shoulder. Each stroke of her hand made him inhale sharply until the fragrance of her hair saturated his senses. God, she might not taste like anything, but she smelled like fresh cut roses.

"I have to have you. Now." She shot the words in his ear while her hands worked together to get the suit down to his thighs. Her mouth burrowed through his hair to find his cheek, and he lifted his head from her shoulder to claim her lips. She kissed him this time, plunging her tongue all the way to the back of his throat before taking a slow journey back out to suck at his bottom lip. The sharp jab of her teeth surprised him, and he pulled away, only to have her bury her hands in his hair to bring him back within reach.

Hell, she only looked fragile, because the strength she used to hold him still while she took his mouth was boggling.

Daniel had to brace his hands against the wall above the woman's shoulders as her kiss threatened to bring him to his knees. She sucked his tongue deep into her mouth then scraped her teeth along the length while releasing it. His dick swelled larger, wanting the same treatment. He pressed against her belly, rolling his hips to let her feel how ready he was.

"Mmm," she purred. "I do enjoy the taste of eagerness."

Her words were odd, but he was too horny to really give a shit about what she said. He needed to be inside her. Either her mouth or her pussy, and he needed to be there now.

Pulling back before she could capture his tongue again, he buried his fingers in her hair and eased her face away. "What's it gonna be, gorgeous? What are you after?"

She smiled, a real smile this time, one that showed all her teeth.

Daniel stared at the sharp fangs no longer hidden behind plump ruby lips. Jesus, a vampire. What were the fucking chances?

"I want it all," she said in a husky tone that shot straight to his groin. "Question is will you let me have it?"

He dragged his gaze to her eyes and smiled while releasing her. She watched with one brow arched high as he finished removing the suit and tossed it aside. "I guess I don't need to ask if you want me to use a condom."

Laughing softly, she shook her head. "That won't be necessary, no." She beckoned him forward with a crooked finger and frowned when he hesitated. "You aren't frightened, are you?"

"That depends." Knowing what she was hadn't dimmed his eagerness. He wasn't sure anything could soften his raging hard-on or dampen the undeniable need to bury himself inside her, it was just the teeth...well...they were a bit intimidating.

"What exactly do you plan to do?" Obviously she was after more than sex here.

She flashed another full smile. "Let me state it in terms you'll have no problem understanding. I'm planning to fuck you while I suck your blood."

The words sent a fresh shot of blood straight to his groin. Holy shit, the guys would never believe this.

Chapter Four

Nadia had expected a much different response than the combination of awe and anticipation she saw before her. She did not necessarily want this lovely young man to fear her, but a show of respect would be nice. Instead, he narrowed his hazel eyes and smirked. It was a look that brought Jason to mind. And with thoughts of Jason, came thoughts of the coven, the master and her exile. Talk about a mood killer.

The best way to ignore the past was to focus on the present. So that's what she did. Fixing her gaze on the man's neck, she offered a slight smirk of her own. "You don't seem all that surprised to have encountered a vampire."

He shrugged one muscular shoulder. "San Francisco is full of freaks."

"Oh really?" Nadia looked into his eyes, and the humor there doused the irritation brought on by such a rude comment. He winked, and despite her best efforts not to, she laughed. "You are quite the devil, aren't you?"

"Oh, you have no idea."

Ooh. She quirked a brow and ran her wet

fingers across his chest. "Is that a threat or a promise?" Water dripped between his pecs and splashed down her forearm as he moved closer. Sliding her arms around his waist, she cupped his ass. The muscles were hard, tight and more than a handful. "Nice," she mumbled.

He kept moving closer until his naked body had her crowded against the rough wooden wall. Not that she was complaining. The feel of his hot skin against her was divine, and he was hot everywhere. His thighs burned hers, his erection singed her belly and his breath warmed her cheek as he lowered his face.

"Speaking of promises." He slid his hands down her sides to wrap them around the backs of her thighs. Without warning, and with impressive ease, he hoisted her off her feet. Instinctively, she released his ass to wrap her arms around his neck and her legs around his waist.

"Are you willing to make me a promise?" he continued.

Nadia nodded while focusing on the close proximity of a very sexy throat. Good Lord, why hadn't she bitten him yet? She licked her lips and leaned closer.

"Promise me you won't take my memory of what's about to happen."

The question diverted her attention. It was not something one would ask unless they'd had more than a passing acquaintance with vampires. She couldn't help but be very intrigued all of a sudden. Where, when and how had this young man ever come into contact with another vampire?

She met his steady gaze. "Why would you assume such a thing?"

"Don't play dumb. Just tell me you won't erase my memories of you."

"Rules are rules…" She stopped and frowned. Who the hell was around to punish her if she broke the rules? But still, detection was the quickest way to annihilation, or so the master liked to preach. It was a hard lesson to ignore after listening to it for one hundred years.

Not willing to say yea or nay to the request, she threaded her hands in his hair and tugged his face close. "We'll see." He scowled, but she kissed the expression away, chuckling at the same time. Once she was through with him, he might not wish to remember everything, and then he'd thank her.

But enough speculating. She was hungry, tired of only thinking about blood and very ready to finally stain her fangs again. Still gripping fistfuls of silky hair, she kissed her way from his mouth, across his chin and down the side of his neck. He cocked his head to the side, silently granting her the permission she hadn't thought to ask for, and she dragged her fangs along his flesh. One thick cord called to her, and without further ado, she parted her lips wide and bit.

The first rush of blood threatened to give her a headache. It was like indulging in a sweet treat too quickly because you feared it might be snatched away. Trying to calm down, she swallowed the next mouthful slower, taking the time to savor the flavor. Whoever this young man was, he lived a clean, healthy life. His blood tasted so pure and fresh, she nearly cried as it brought to mind her lost servants. What were the chances that the first person she tapped would be so satisfying?

If asked twenty-four hours ago, she would have laughed and sworn the outside had nothing this good to offer. Why else set up a coven where vampires could regulate what their servants ate and drank? Why else obsess about the purity and cleanliness of the mortal blood surrounding them? Why do any of that if the outside world was overrun with men such as the one pulsing delightfully into her mouth? It certainly made a girl wonder, and she was tempted to lure others out of the coven and away from the controlling master with the promise of sweeter things. Ha! Wouldn't that just boil his blood.

Another rich swallow was all it took to bring her thoughts back to her meal. Such a meal deserved her undivided attention, after all. But as glorious as it tasted, she hadn't forgotten the hard body pressed against her. In fact, it seemed the more she drank from the young man, the more restless he became. His heart pounded loudly, his pulse raced and he rocked his hips between her legs, teasing her with the head of his cock. Didn't he realize all he had to do was ask?

Unwilling to let go of the accommodating artery she'd latched on to, Nadia blindly ran her hand down between their bodies until she could curl her fingers around his persistent erection. For a moment, it seemed his heart stopped and his blood ceased to flow, but then in a great rush, he filled her mouth while thrusting against her palm. A combination of water and pre-cum made it almost impossible to grip him as he slicked back and forth within her hand. When his breathing became labored and the flavor of his blood turned very familiar, she shifted against him to fit the head of his cock against her opening. He pushed inside with a low grunt, filling her with everything he had.

Nadia eased her fangs from his skin, and swallowed the blood that remained in her mouth. Keeping her face nestled against the warmth of his neck, she closed her eyes and absorbed the heavenly feel of his hard shaft pumping into her.

The wooden wall was rough and unforgiving at her back, and the water splashed off his shoulder to sting her eyes, but she'd gladly tolerate worse given how bloody excellent the sex felt. She'd never been a woman easily satisfied, but this young man seemed to know just the right way to fill her. He teased the limits of her womb with every forward thrust and made her want to scream with each withdrawal, but he was quick to fill her again before she could voice a single protest.

"Fucking water." He mumbled the words over her head then the water ceased to rain down. If not for the inability to speak, Nadia would have thanked him.

No longer worried about being splashed in the eyes, she lifted her head to rest it against the wall and took great delight in watching the play of muscles along her lover's sexy shoulders and chest. There was no hair to distract from the golden perfection of his skin, and she couldn't stop herself from spreading her hands across his pecs.

Beneath her right palm, his heart beat out a violent rhythm. Hunger swelled within her. There was nothing sweeter than the taste of blood while a lover climaxed, and this man was moving closer and closer with every thump of his heart. Curling her hands up over his shoulders, she held on tight and once more aimed for his neck. He swore as she sank her fangs in, but she knew it wasn't pain that caused the reaction.

"I sure hope you can drink and come at the same time, gorgeous." The words were a low growl in her ear, and the accent she'd heard earlier was a bit stronger.

Nadia flexed her inner muscles to prove she could and was rewarded with a sexy chuckle and a rather aggressive thrust. She gasped and instinctively bit deeper.

"Easy there," he warned. "It won't go over too well if I show up for work bruised and battered looking."

No mark would remain from her bite, but clearly he didn't know that much about vampires. Still, she eased up a bit, worried that an intense orgasm might cause her to do unintentional damage. Normal bites closed up and vanished quickly, but it would take slightly longer if she accidentally ripped his skin off. For good measure, she gave him a quick lick before sucking more blood from him.

"Mmm," he moaned. "Do that again."

She licked him again, and he bucked against her so hard the wooden surround shook and water dripped from the shower head. A few drops splashed onto her cheek and ran toward her mouth to mix with the blood. While wondering why she'd always turned her nose up at watered down blood, her orgasm hit.

Tearing her teeth free, Nadia screamed as the climax worked its way from her core outward. Her body tingled inside and out, burning hot everywhere her skin touched mortal flesh. Maybe it was because she'd grown accustomed to her existence within the coven, or maybe it was because she'd known no other men but her servants for the last five years but something was very different about the way she felt at this moment.

"Holy Mother of God." The rough words poured in her ear as she felt the final throb of their joint orgasm ebb. "Holy shit," he mumbled on a shaky breath.

Nadia couldn't help but laugh, but she did so with very little energy and the sound barely escaped the sweaty curve of the man's neck. Gracious, she hoped she possessed the energy to wipe his memories away.

"You have to let me remember this." It was as if he could read her mind.

Nadia lifted her heavy head and met his glazed over expression. Dear Lord, talk about the "just been fucked" look. His lashes eclipsed his eyes, his cheeks were flushed and his lips parted to allow him to drag in deep breaths of air. And if all that weren't sexy enough, and she believed it might be, his hair feathered across his forehead and teased the bridge of his nose. The dripping strands looked much darker than they had when she first laid eyes on him, and the deeper shade turned his nondescript hazel eyes black.

Gracious, he was lovely, and she regretted not exchanging names. Was it too late? Would he willingly meet her right here, night after night, to let her feed? And how long would it take before he offered himself completely—

"Well?"

Nadia blinked then frowned, realizing she'd forgotten the question. "Well what?" Their entwined position was fast becoming uncomfortable, and a subtle wiggle was all it took to have him release her. She got her feet under her but leaned heavily against the wall. Sex had never taken so much out of her.

"Are you going to let me remember this?"

"I don't know yet." Which was true. Despite no one being around, she was still wary to break the rules, but the longer she stared at his face, the more willing she was to risk it.

"Mind if I get dressed while you think about it?" There was more than a hint of irritation in his voice as he turned and began gathering his clothes. Foregoing the swimsuit, he merely pulled his shorts and tank on. He glanced back at her while slicking his hands through his wet hair. The action plastered it back off his forehead, giving his features a more mature appearance than the shaggy fringe of bangs had.

Looking at him now made her wonder how old he was, and if she had to guess, she'd say no older than Jason's twenty-two years. What was it with her and the young ones? Jason had certainly proved they weren't all that easy to train, but there was the boundless energy and fantastic physiques, both of which this man possessed in spades.

"It's never a good sign if a woman thinks about something this long."

Nadia met his irritated gaze. "It's better for both of us if I do what I'm supposed to do. It wouldn't be safe if you bragged to your friends about getting lucky with a vampire."

He looked offended. "You assume I would brag?"

"You're a man, it's in your nature." He was smart enough not to deny the claim, and she admired him for it. "I'm sorry, really I am, but things are the way they are for a reason." Dear God, she sounded like the master now. He'd be so proud.

The man who had just given her probably the best sex she'd ever had, stood before her with his nose cocked in the air and his arms spread. "Fine, just do it then."

Nadia fought a smile. "It won't hurt, and I do not have to touch you." Regardless of what she said, she pushed away from the wall to step closer. Just one last time, she wanted to feel the heat of his body and the smooth texture of his skin.

Laying her hand in the center of his chest, she inhaled sharply. Such an innocent gesture and yet it made her want to curl around him and take everything he had to offer again. Wow, time to erase his memories and get out of here while she still had her sanity.

"Just close your eyes and relax." Advice she would do well to take it seemed.

Before obeying, he stared at her long and hard. "I might not forget you, you know?"

She concentrated on the subtle sound of his heart and the fragrance of his blood. Her mouth watered as her gaze fell to the side of his neck. As predicted, the wound she'd inflicted was gone, just as his memories of her would be. Would it comfort him to know she would never forget him?

She held his gaze, memorizing the mixture of green, brown and gold then she dropped her focus to his mouth and the kiss-swollen lips. What if she did not find anyone else who tasted as good or was as willing? What if erasing his memories ended any hope she had to survive this exile? What if. What if. What if.

Nadia swallowed a growl and silently ordered herself just to do it.

"Part of me hopes you do remember," she said very quietly, but his eyes widened. Seconds later, she reached into his thoughts to erase what they'd shared.

Chapter Five

It had taken Nadia the rest of the night to recover from her encounter with the stranger on the beach, so she waited until the following night to seek out Sera. As planned, she began her search at Captive Fantasy. Aside from knowing Sera's lover, Valentino, was the owner, she knew only that the place used to be some sort of sex club. Lord only knew what she'd find once she got there, but strangely the thought of sex only made her think of last night and the young man she'd let slip away.

Such thoughts were not only annoying but anti-productive.

Focusing on the task at hand, she arrived at Captive Fantasy and stepped to the end of a very long line. The women directly in front of her turned to give her a thorough once over, their expressions quickly becoming hostile.

Nadia wanted to hiss at them. She'd dressed with special care, not wanting to seem too sexy or too meek, hence the plain, navy, T-shirt dress and cowboy boots. Though perhaps these women were just irritated because not too sexy and not too meek worked on her. Clearly they felt the need to dress as cheap whores, but it wasn't worth the energy to slip into their minds to read their pathetic thoughts.

"Hello." Nadia would play nice for now if it meant gaining information, and luckily these women had the look of regulars. "This is my first time here so I'm not sure what to expect." She added a full smile, hoping it looked innocent. Interacting with women was not exactly high on the list of things she excelled at. They normally took one look at her and hated her, which was fine. Men were more fun, anyway.

One woman huffed. "It's a strip club so you should expect to see men stripping." The other women snickered.

Nadia maintained her smile. "You're right, how silly of me." With that, she stepped out of line and walked straight to the front where a large man stood guard at the entrance. Every few minutes, he pushed open the door to let a lucky woman or two slip inside. His gaze skimmed over Nadia, and she offered another radiant smile.

"You need to wait in line just like all the others," he told her without even really looking at her.

"Would it make a difference if I told you I know the owner?" Not that she really expected Valentino to vouch for her. He hadn't been at the coven for very long, but long enough for her to sense they'd probably never be friends.

The doorman glanced at her and shook his head. "Every single woman in this line claims to know the owner, sweetheart."

Nadia scowled. If only the stubborn man would look at her for longer than a half second. Perhaps the direct approach would work best here.

"Are you paid to be rude?" That got his undivided attention.

He met her gaze, arched a coal black brow and unknowingly fell prey to good old-fashioned, vampire mind control. Pleased with herself, Nadia sauntered past the captivated man and straight into the club. Women bitched and moaned as the door swung shut, and she wondered how the doorman would explain what had just happened.

"Need a table, or are you meeting friends?" The question came from the gloriously handsome man positioned right inside the door. He had all the overbearing presence of his coworker outside and none of the clothes. Before she could finish gawking at the tiny black shorts hugging his hips, he grabbed her left hand and stamped the top with the letters CF.

Nadia stared at the blurry red ink. "Um...actually, I need to speak to Valentino." She lifted her gaze to the man's amused face. Great, no doubt that was another thing every woman in this place had said at one point or another. "Listen," she continued before he could make some snide comment to that effect. "If you tell him Nadia from Santa Fe is here, he'll tell you he knows me." Maybe. She hoped.

The man studied her from behind a silky curtain of dark blond bangs. The longer he stalled, the more tempted Nadia was to simply force him to do her will, but she wasn't here to draw undue attention to herself and the more people she used her powers on, the more likely she was to get noticed. But if this guy didn't make up his mind soon...

Finally, he tucked a few strands of hair behind his ear and nodded. "All right. Stay here, and I'll see what Val has to say."

He strolled away from his post, granting Nadia a wonderful opportunity to see how wonderful his ass looked in the shorts that left very little to the imagination. In fact, they were almost as small as the swimsuit...no! She refused to think of him.

Left alone and determined not to lose focus by thinking about last night, Nadia wandered deeper into the club. Tables were scattered about with no clear walkway from the door to the stage. Men, dressed in the same black shorts as the doorman, weaved in and out of the tables delivering drinks and accepting tips. From what she could see, they were all equally gorgeous but very different. It seemed Captive Fantasy was all about diversity and quality.

Her gaze settled on a tall, platinum haired waiter as he leaned over a table full of giggling women. He had the body of a Greek statue and the face of a male model. Nice, very nice. Her fangs ached and her mouth watered as she considered what he might taste like. Last night's delicious feast had only heightened her need for blood, and this place teemed with prospects.

Good naturally the waiter sidestepped one woman's attempt to pinch his ass and blew a kiss at the entire table before strolling away. Catching Nadia's stare, he winked. Even from across the club, she could see how blue his eyes were. Wow.

If not for the sudden hush that fell over the crowd and the building pulse of music, Nadia would have gladly kept her gaze fixed on the gorgeous waiter. But the charged atmosphere drew her attention to the stage where a man stood silhouetted in the center. Something stirred inside her as she studied the outline of powerful shoulders, trim hips and muscular thighs. If she weren't mistaken—the music grew louder, the lights brightened and she swallowed a gasp. It couldn't be. And yet there was no mistaking the man from the beach as the lights washed over him and the crowd erupted with shrieks.

Oh my God.

Nadia stared with the rest of the hoard, thinking she'd never seen anything so perfect. He was dressed all in white, setting off the sun-bleached highlights of his hair along with the golden hue of his skin. When he smiled, his teeth seemed to match the baggy pants and flowy tunic. The smile stayed firmly in place as he began to move to the pulsating music. The beat sounded Latin, and it was so infectious, her hips instinctively began to sway.

The tunic came off, and Nadia froze. The lights illuminated the muscles she'd touched just last night and all that hot skin she couldn't stop thinking about. Focusing on the brown discs around his nipples, her throat went dry. Oh God. As hard as it was, she dragged her gaze downward, following the defined cut of his abs straight to the top of his pants.

The pants sat incredibly low on his hips, held on by a dangling drawstring. Captivated, she watched the cord swish back and forth across the apex of his thighs. Knowing what he looked like naked only heightened the torment.

Glancing around, she realized every woman stared at the stage with raw hunger shining in their eyes. The sight provoked feelings of possessiveness that annoyed and confused her. It was one thing to hate the queen for taking the master from her and another to despise Pepper for wanting to get her claws into Chase, but the urge to cloak this crowd in a wave of uncomfortable power made no sense. The man on stage was nothing to her. Yes, his blood had been delicious and his body an absolute gift, but neither of those things made him hers.

As true as that was, she still wanted to do something horrible to every woman watching him as if he were their next meal.

"What are you doing here?"

Nadia whipped around and came face to face with Valentino, who was just as unbelievably gorgeous as she recalled. His sable hair flopped over one eye in a rather rakish manner, drawing attention to the cut of his cheekbone and the fullness of his mouth. Too bad his sexy lips were set in a tight line and the one brown eye she could see was full of loathing. The open hostility on his face amused her enough to momentarily forget the show onstage.

"Valentino, how lovely to see you," she purred, all honey and sugar. His expression darkened, but it didn't deter her. "I knew you'd agree to see me."

"I came out here to tell you to leave." He crossed his arms, drawing her attention to the interesting outfit he wore. Tight, black, leather pants showcased his wonderful lower physique while a black, leather vest did little to mask the perfection of his upper body. A few women at a nearby table stared rather openly as opposed to watching the ongoing performance.

Nadia dragged her gaze down then back up, slowly, so as to enjoy the journey. "Shouldn't you ask why I'm here before you demand I leave?"

"I don't care why you're here. I only care how quick you can be gone."

"What did I ever do to you to deserve such a cold welcome?" She crossed her arms to mimic his stubborn stance.

"Women like you are all about what you would do if given the chance."

"Ha! As if it's fair to judge me in such a way. Not once did I interfere with your stay at the coven." Which was true. Sure she'd looked her fill and maybe wondered what it would be like to have sex with this gorgeous man, but thinking and looking were not crimes.

Valentino sighed. "You have ten seconds to tell me why you're here."

"I need to see Sera."

"No." With that, he actually turned as if to leave her.

Nadia grabbed his arm and struggled to stop him. "Wait a goddamn minute. I need to see Sera, and I'll find her even if you don't help me."

He turned, fixing her with a truly hostile glare. "Don't go anywhere near her. She wants nothing to do with the coven or anything associated with it. I'm sure you can understand why."

"Fine, whatever, but I have nothing to do with the coven anymore. They are not why I'm here."

"You expect me to believe that coming from the master's lapdog?" He snorted and arched a brow. "Please give me a little credit, Nadia, for being able to sniff out a lie."

"Well, obviously you haven't perfected that little talent because it's the honest truth." She released him to prop her hands on her hips. "If you must know, I've been exiled." God, would she ever be able to say that without feeling the pain and anger all over again?

"Exiled? You? For what?" He shook his head and held up a hand. "No, don't answer that. Let me guess." After looking her up and down, he chuckled and met her gaze. "My God, you sniffed after the master one too many times, didn't you?"

"Does it matter?" It still did not seem fair to be cast out and punished for feelings she had no control over.

Valentino's chuckle turned to a full laugh. "Yeah, it matters."

"Fine," Nadia huffed. "If you must know the gory details. I refused to swear fealty to that bitch of a queen."

"Whoa." Valentino whistled softly. "I'm surprised you were only exiled. The master must care for you a great deal because I got the impression he'd kill for much less than that."

Nadia opened her mouth to voice some scathing retort, but stopped. Could it be? Was it possible the master had shown mercy by exiling her?

"So, why do you need to see Sera?" Valentino's question shattered Nadia's wandering thoughts.

"Isn't that obvious? She left the safety of the coven voluntarily, and I want to know how she survives. I need her help, I guess you could say."

"So you're willing to survive on synthetic blood and give up all the benefits you enjoyed with your servants?"

Nadia couldn't resist shooting a glance toward the stage. Once she did, she couldn't look away. The pants were gone now, leaving the young man clad in the smallest excuse for a pair of underwear she'd ever seen. They were made of white mesh and left absolutely nothing to the imagination. He sauntered to the edge of the stage, his hips rolling to the saucy tempo of the music, and the drooling women shrieked like a flock of annoying birds.

"Don't even entertain the thought of putting your fangs anywhere near one of my guys."

Nadia somehow pulled her attention back to Valentino. All the earlier anger and dislike was back in his eyes. "What is his name?"

"Didn't you just hear what I said?"

"I'm not deaf, Valentino." She glanced at the stage. "Where's the harm in telling me his name, or maybe I could just ask one of these women—"

"Daniel," he snarled. "And leave him the fuck alone."

"He looks like he's old enough to make his own decisions." A low growl was her only warning before Valentino snatched her arm and tugged her toward him.

He lowered his face and bared his fangs. "I won't let you turn any of my guys into food, Nadia."

Despite the fierce pressure of his bruising grip, she managed to keep her expression steady. "I never mistreated my servants, and if asked, they'd tell you how happy I made them."

"None of my guys will ever be your servant." He yanked her a bit closer. "Do I make myself clear?"

Nadia couldn't resist taking advantage of how close their bodies were. She smiled and slid a leg between Valentino's leather-clad thighs, but he released her before she could brush against anything fun.

"This isn't a game, Nadia. Leave my guys alone."

The music ended, setting off a loud cacophony of clapping and yelling. She glanced at the stage and watched Daniel disappear into the shadowy wings. "What if it's too late?"

"What did you just say?"

She knew better than to repeat herself. Shrugging, she turned back to Valentino. "Will you or won't you let me see Sera?"

"There's nothing either of us can do for you, Nadia. You made this bed, and only you can lie in it." With that annoying bit of wisdom, he stalked away.

Well then. Now what the hell was she supposed to do?

****

It was pathetically simple for Nadia to make her way backstage, and Valentino was a fool to think she'd give up so easily. Though it was not Sera she was currently searching for. Once she wiped the memories clean of each person who saw her, she concentrated on finding Daniel. Easier said than done, it seemed.

The hallway was lined with closed doors, and each one was marked with initials. Unfortunately, the letter D appeared to be very popular. After eliminating the first two doors, by way of instinct and her extraordinary sense of smell, she halted before the third and inhaled the familiar fragrance of coconuts. Bingo. The scent wasn't as strong as it had been on the beach, but no amount of sweat could hide it from her. Without a doubt, she'd found him.

As she reached for the knob, unwilling to knock and risk being turned away, she once more regretted having erased his memories. This would be easier if the sex they'd had was as fresh in his head as it was in hers. Just his smell was enough to stir her insides and soak her panties, not to mention the promise of his blood. Aroused, anxious and a little wary, she moistened her lips and opened the door.

At first, she feared the room was empty then she caught the sound of the shower and the low hum of a masculine voice attempting to sing. Daniel's inability to carry a tune seemed strange given how well he moved on stage. She listened to a few more off-key notes, trying to figure out what song it might be. Finally she gave up and turned her attention to the room. There was no easier way to get a feel for a man than to root around in his things. Yes, it was a bit underhanded, but it had served her well in the past.

She closed the door and headed toward an unzipped duffel bag tossed onto a black futon. Inside, she found an array of cd's, a cell phone, a magazine called "Surf" and a change of clothes. Hmm. So much for discovering the secrets of Daniel, the Captive Fantasy dancer. She'd suspected the very first time she'd seen him he was a surfer, so it was actually more of a surprise to discover he was a stripper.

Disappointed by what the duffel bag had yielded, she folded the camouflage cargo shorts and shoved them back inside just as the shower turned off. The humming stopped as well, and before long, the room filled with humid moisture. Turning, she found Daniel framed in the doorway, wearing a very shocked expression and a loosely knotted white towel.

It was lovely to discover he was just as adorable as he'd looked in the moonlight. More so, actually. The lights in the room were harsh and fluorescent, the kind that illuminated flaws as opposed to covering them, but Daniel had none.

"Hello, Daniel."

He narrowed his eyes and swept his gaze over her. "Do I know you?"

She wanted to tell him that he knew her as intimately as he possibly could, but she held her tongue. Best to just start over. "Um, not really." That made his full lips pull into a frown. "But I'm more than willing to let you get to know me.

The smirk he'd flashed last night, the one that reminded her of Jason, transformed his features, and his eyes danced. "I see you're going for the direct approach. Most of the women just wait out back and accost me on the way to my car."

"And does that work for them?"

He shrugged and tucked the edge of the towel in so he could let it go. "Sometimes it does, yeah. It depends."

"On?" She couldn't help that she was curious. She wanted to know what made Daniel tick. She needed to know, because the moment Valentino had turned his back on her, she'd decided the only way to survive was to acquire the two things she needed more than anything else. Blood and sex. Upon reaching that conclusion, Daniel had been the only one to come to mind. She liked the way he tasted, she loved the way he felt, so why the hell not grant him the honor of becoming her new servant?

It all made extraordinary sense to her.

Daniel chuckled and leaned back against the bathroom door. With his hands shoved behind his back and his gaze steady on her face, he continued to smile. "I guess it depends on what they look like and what they are after."

"I see. And how would I do, if I were to accost you in such a fashion?" She held her arms out to give him an unrestricted view of her simple outfit.

Clearly the intent to look innocent and

harmless had been wasted on Valentino, and as Daniel studied her, she wished she were dressed in something a great deal sexier. Nothing as extreme as the glittery mini-skirts and cheap heels she'd seen on the other women, but a short, black, halter-dress would be nice, perhaps with her silver heels.

"I can't answer without knowing what you're after."

"Let's just assume I want what the other women always want." She licked her lips and trailed her gaze down the line of his damp torso. God, he was delicious. She wanted to taste him now, fresh from the shower, with none of the cloying flavor of the beach to get in the way. Her fangs ached with the desire to do so.

"Is that all you want though? Just fast, meaningless sex?"

Hmm. She did not quite enjoy the idea of him having fast, meaningless sex with a number of strange women night after night. Frowning, she lifted her gaze to his face. The smirk was gone, and his eyes no longer danced. In fact, his expression was eerily serious, as if her answer mattered a great deal.

"To be honest, I never enjoyed my sex fast and meaningless." He arched a brow, but she continued before he could speak. "In fact, I prefer the sex I have to last all night long, until the sun decides to come up and the approaching day can no longer be denied."

"I see." His voice had dropped an octave or

two.

"So, knowing that, would you or wouldn't you allow me to accost you?" Nadia lost patience with having nearly the full width of the room between them and slowly approached Daniel. He stood his ground, even kept his hands behind his back, but his gaze was steady and watchful. His smell hit her like a sharp slap across the face the moment she'd halved the distance between them.

Halting, she inhaled the exotic combination of coconuts, musk and arousal. She smiled and glanced down to see the towel no longer laid as flat as it had a moment ago. "I think the answer you're looking for is, yes."

With no warning, he reached for her and pulled her the rest of the way toward him. Their bodies crashed together, and she dropped her head back with a gasp of real surprise. It was not often anyone caught her unaware, and part of her buzzed with the thrill of being dominated, while another part seethed at her show of weakness.

"Tell me your name, because somehow you obviously know mine." He searched her face, still wearing the super serious expression.

"Valentino let it slip while warning me away from you."

"Just me?"

Nadia shook her head and lowered her gaze to Daniel's mouth. "No, all of his guys are off limits to me."

"And why is that?" While he asked, he eased his grip on her arms to rub his hands up and down her flesh. The short sleeves of the dress were pushed to her shoulders with each upward stroke.

"Your boss doesn't trust me." She laid her hand over his heart and absorbed the force of the beat into her palm. His skin was even warmer than it had been last night.

"How do you know one another, and you still haven't told me your name." He cocked her chin up to look in her eyes.

"He and I have mutual acquaintances." It seemed the easiest way to explain, at least for now. "As for my name. Nadia."

"Ah, Nadia." Her skin tingled as he said her name in the same light accent that had filled her ear last night. "I was convinced I'd never see you again."

Chapter Six

Daniel could taste Nadia's shock in her kiss. Did the little vixen really think she was that forgettable? If so, she underestimated good old fashion willpower. He hadn't wanted to forget her, and thanks to the fact his boss happened to be a vampire, he knew how to sidestep a few of their tricks.

Nadia began to struggle against him, and fearing she might sink her fangs into his tongue, he ended the kiss and pulled back. Her eyes flashed as she lifted her lashes to glare at him. She had such gorgeous, silver eyes. He'd dreamt of them last night. Along with the rest of her.

After swiping the back of her hand across her mouth, she locked gazes with him. "You and I have never met." The conviction in her tone was adorable.

Daniel chuckled. "Oh yes, not only have we met, but I seem to recall the exact sound you make right before you—"

"Enough!" With a little huff, she pushed away from him and turned to stalk across the room. "I don't understand." She mumbled it more to herself than to him and shook her head again. "My powers have never failed me."

"Nadia." She ignored him while continuing to pace and mumble. "Nadia," he said a bit louder.

She stopped and turned. "What?"

"I didn't want to forget you." For a second, her features softened, making him wonder if hearing that pleased her. "It isn't your fault that the memory erase didn't work, so stop beating yourself up."

"My powers should be stronger than your resistance."

"Why? Because you say so? Or is it written in some ancient book somewhere?" Her holier than thou, vampire attitude could get old really fast. She needed to know he wasn't just some insignificant mortal. "It really burns you up that I remembered, doesn't it?"

She scowled and turned her back on him. "Shut up."

Daniel swallowed the urge to laugh out loud. "If you wanted me to forget, why are you here?"

To say he'd been shocked to see her would be a huge understatement. But at the same time, one glance had quickened his heartbeat while shooting blood straight to his groin. He wasn't sure it really mattered why she was here, as long as she planned on staying.

"I did not know you worked here, so I assure you, I did not come here to see you." She kept her back to him as she answered.

"Did you see my performance?" The slight

stiffening of her spine was all the answer he needed. Smiling, he pushed away from the door and crept up behind her. Of course, she heard him and turned long before he reached her. Her deepening scowl made him smile. "Did you enjoy it?"

"I did not tell you whether I even saw it or not."

"But we both know you did."

She arched a brow. "Oh, so now you can read minds, too?"

Before he could assure her that he could do a lot of things but reading minds wasn't one of them, a strange look passed over her face. The anger seeped from her eyes, replaced by something that looked alarmingly like pain.

"Are you okay?" He reached for her, but she stumbled away from him, wrapping her arms around herself and emitting a low, pitiful moan. Concern lanced through Daniel.

"Nadia?" He caught her as she crumbled and eased her down until he was sitting on the floor with her curled in his lap. Holding her as he was, he could feel the shivers wracking her body. "Talk to me, gorgeous."

Moaning again, she buried her face against his chest and wrapped her arms around his body. She was cold enough to make him really worry, and whatever was happening seemed far more serious than blood lust. Maybe he should send for Valentino?

"I don't feel good." The words were almost

too quiet to hear, and her breath barely registered against his chest.

"Tell me what's wrong so I can help." He shifted her in his arms in order to lift her face. Her eyes were glazed over and shiny with unshed tears. "Are you ill? Do you need blood?" If it was within his power to give her what she needed, he'd do so without hesitation.

Under different circumstances, the silent vow might have shocked, or even terrified him. After all, he was only twenty-three, and the last thing he was looking for was a relationship. And yet...all the things he didn't think he wanted seemed sort of possible with Nadia. Not only was she the complete opposite of what he normally attracted, it felt really good and really right to hold her. He might not know why, but he knew he wanted to be the one to comfort her.

Was he having the moment people speak of when they realize the love of their life is right in front of them? He didn't know, but maybe it wouldn't be so bad if that was exactly what was happening.

Nadia's quiet sobbing brought his thoughts back into focus, and his heart broke as tears ran unchecked down her pale cheeks. "Whatever it is, tell me how to make it go away." Why wouldn't she talk to him? What the hell was wrong?

She shook her head and buried her face against his chest again. Her tears soaked his skin, but he didn't care. "Nadia, I want to help."

He couldn't recall the last time he'd felt so damn helpless and desperate. "I swear to God, I'll do anything."

****

Nadia had never felt so forlorn. Even as her mortal self had died to make way for her transformation, she hadn't experienced this level of emptiness. It felt as if someone or something ripped at her heart with merciless claws, while the rest of her body wept to be consumed and filled like only her servants could. Tears continued to stream down her cheeks, and realization hit.

They were lost to her.

This pain, longing and emptiness could only mean her bond with her servants had been severed. Whether they had found new mistresses or simply fed from the master, she didn't know and it didn't matter. They were gone, never to be hers again. The coven, and all it represented, was truly lost to her now. A reality that brought fresh tears and did nothing to ease the discomfort burning through her.

Daniel held her in his strong arms, running his hand up and down her spine and whispering soothing words against her hair. He wanted to help her. He'd do anything, give her anything, she need only say the words.

Her mind and body screamed at her to replace what she'd lost. It was the only way to heal, the only way to gather the strength to move on. And she needed to move on. She refused to lose sight of her determination to thrive. Daniel had offered, and to end the misery, she'd gladly take.

It was easy enough to twist within Daniel's embrace to straddle his lap and even easier to tug the towel's knot free. As it parted to reveal the semi-hard length of his penis, he cupped her chin and lifted her face. She couldn't let him ask the question she saw in his eyes, so she silenced him with a harsh kiss full of tongue, fangs and unrestrained hunger. It did not take long for her to taste blood.

Sucking the sweet substance from Daniel's tongue, Nadia wrapped her fingers around his cock and worked him to a full erection. He moaned, shifted his hips and tried to free his tongue from her fangs. More blood filled her mouth as she resisted his efforts. Every drop eased the ache inside her, but it would take so much more to fully extinguish it.

The master had offered to spare her this agony as if he had known the degree of pain awaiting her. Why had she refused him? What a fool she'd been to believe it wouldn't be so bad, to believe that holding back her heart from her servants would protect her from the pain of separation.

Good Lord, what if she had actually allowed herself to fall in love with them? How many vampires had died from losing their servants? Maybe being exiled was not the real threat here, and if the master believed she loved her servants, did he also believe this moment would destroy her? If so—

Daniel worked his tongue free with a curse, ending the path of Nadia's thoughts. Pulling back, he cupped her face in a tight grip that demanded her full attention.

"If it's blood you need, just ask, for Christ's sake. No need to rip my fucking tongue in half."

If she survived this night with her sanity intact, she'd apologize for her rough handling, but right now she had no choice but to let her body take what it needed.

Without a word, Nadia shifted her focus to the fluttering pulse at the base of Daniel's throat. In her current state, it would be foolish and dangerous to feed from such a rich source, and yet she couldn't tear her gaze away. He swallowed, tightening the cords on either side of his neck and unknowingly sealing his fate.

Moistening her lips, she struck with blinding speed.

Her fangs pierced Daniel's throat, and blood gushed into her mouth. His soft mew of discomfort was enough to rein her in, and she eased the pressure of her bite while reaching for his thoughts to dull the pain. He fought against her power, until they reached a silent compromise of sorts. Fine, if he wanted it to hurt a little, where was the harm?

Once she consumed enough blood to take the edge off her hunger and ease some of the emptiness, her focus shifted. Her body still craved sex in its rawest, truest form, and she began to stroke Daniel's cock once more, dragging her hand from root to tip while sucking lightly at his throat. She wasn't willing to abandon the taste of his blood just yet, but she no longer fed as if he was the last thing between her and destruction.

"Nadia...my God..." Daniel's husky words filled her ear, making her flex her fingers around his cock. A hiss of pleasure followed, and he grabbed hold of her wrist, forcing her grip to stop once it reached the base. Uncoiling her fingers, he guided her hand toward his balls, silently showing her exactly what he wanted.

Nadia obliged and cupped the weight of Daniel's sac. His pulse increased, as did the pace at which she drank. At this rate, she'd have to stop soon or things could quickly get out of control.

Daniel spread his legs as far open as her position across his hips would allow. "Jesus, you keep that up, I'm going to come." He began to move his hips, which brushed his balls across her palm and dragged his cock along her forearm. Telltale signs of excitement dripped from the head to moisten her skin, but she refused to stop.

"Take me inside, Nadia. For God's sake, let me fuck you." He bucked harder, and she lost her grip on his balls and nearly the hold she had on his throat. He tore at her dress, pushing the hem above her waist while somehow clawing at her panties at the same time. Fabric ripped, his fingers found her opening, and he pushed one deep inside, causing her muscles to contract hard. All the while, his blood grew hotter and tastier.

Nadia prided herself on never having lost control in all her years as a vampire, and yet now she hung on as if suspended by a weak thread. Caution screamed at her to release Daniel just as he shoved two more fingers inside her. She swallowed a hot serving of his blood to stifle a moan, and the potency shot straight to her groin, adding to the already unbearable pleasure of Daniel's fingers working inside her.

The orgasm that followed took her completely off guard, and she ceased drinking lest she choke. Wave after wave of pleasure hit her as Daniel pumped his fingers in and out. Keeping her face buried at his throat, she let the smell of his blood add to the moment, every so often flicking her tongue out for just a little taste.

Eventually, the contractions faded away, allowing her to think again, and if she could think she could certainly feed. Before Daniel could even slip his hand free, she was back at his throat.

"Not sure how much blood I have left, gorgeous." The words teased, but his tone held a hint of real concern. Despite that, he nudged at her sex with the head of his cock. "Open for me." One more push put him inside, but her recent orgasm made their joining a slick, tight struggle.

"Fuck. Fuck. Fuck." Every curse was accompanied by a hard push, until he filled her completely. Wrapping his arms around her, he collapsed onto his back, taking her along. The shift in position forced her away from his throat long enough to make her snarl with frustration, but then he cocked his head to the side in an open invitation.

Nadia drank and drank while Daniel held her hips steady to receive his rhythmic thrusts. It was hard to say which of them began to breathe faster or louder, as another orgasm built within her. The taste of his blood carried the approach of his climax as well, and the spicy flavor set off a burning in her veins she'd never felt before.

Of course, she'd fed while her servants climaxed, but not once had it tasted like this. Daniel's blood burned her throat on the way down and continued its fiery path through her veins. She'd read stories about vampires experiencing this sensation but chalked such things up to nothing more than myth and legend. But it was real. Very real.

Daniel's thrusts grew fiercer. "Oh my God," he moaned.

Arching, he cocked his head back, stretching his neck against her lips. Another moan brought on the strong pulse of his release and a powerful rush of blood into her mouth. The combination made Nadia's head spin, and she sucked long and hard at his neck while he shuddered beneath her.

Imprisoned by renewed hunger, she continued to feed long after Daniel's body calmed, and even after his skin grew cold and his hands fell from her hips, she couldn't bring herself to stop. Something, but who knew exactly what, triggered the warning bells in her mind, and she ripped her mouth from his throat to look at his face. His eyes drifted shut, a sigh slipped from his lips and his entire body went limp.

"No!" Oh God, how could she be stupid enough to take too much, to risk his life?

Terrified that the unthinkable had happened, she tore her wrist open and smeared the wound over Daniel's lips. They were warm against her skin, calming some of the panic in her heart. After a few dismayed sounds, Daniel flicked his tongue against her wrist then began to drink with a show of hunger that pleased and startled all at once. With every drag from her vein, his teeth gripped a little tighter, and she pulled free before he could take too much.

The world certainly did not need another vampire.

She'd given Daniel just enough blood to make sure he would be all right, and color slowly crept back into his face. Still, she kept a close watch on his features while licking the wound closed at her wrist.

After a few moments, Daniel opened his eyes and winked at her. "How come I didn't get dessert the first time we had sex?" His voice was surprisingly strong and steady.

Frowning, she ignored the humor. "Tell me how you feel?"

Aside from being covered in a shiny layer of sweat, he looked more than all right. A quick glance at his throat showed the wound closing just as it should. Perhaps her panic had been for nothing. Was it possible he'd been fully conscious the entire time her wrist had been at his mouth? If so, it meant he'd willingly taken her blood. Could he possibly have any idea what the consequences of that were?

"I feel tired, drained, a bit sore and unbelievably satisfied." He winked again and resettled his hands at her hips. "And how do you feel?"

"At peace." The words slipped out before she could stop them.

"Good." Daniel's wide smile pleased her but also drew her gaze to his mouth.

"You have blood on your lips." Before he could speak, she leaned down to kiss away the evidence of what she'd given him. He turned away at the last moment, and her efforts were wasted.

Nadia straightened and stared into his suddenly serious face. "What is wrong?"

"You said you feel at peace now, but I need to know what was wrong earlier." He moved her off his lap so he could sit up. The towel remained spread underneath him, and it didn't seem to occur to him that his nakedness might be a distraction. "You looked as if you were in pain?"

"I would rather not talk about it." Nadia brought her knees to her chest and wrapped her arms around her legs. "What we did has made me feel better, and I promise you'll never see me so weak again." She peeked through her lashes to catch his frown. Now did not seem like a good time to mention the consequences of him taking her blood.

"You don't have to apologize for having a weak moment, and I didn't mind being here to help you through it. That's my job as the guy, right? To hold you when you're afraid—"

"I didn't say I was afraid." But she had been, and obviously, he was more perceptive than she'd imagined.

Daniel reached for her, and she allowed the embrace. His heart was a nice steady beat under her ear as she snuggled against his chest. Thank God, she hadn't killed him, but she'd keep that moment of horror to herself. There was no reason Daniel need know how close he'd been to death.

"Hey?" He eased back to see her face. "Are you willing to stick around while I take another shower? I'm starving to death, and I'd rather not eat here."

Nadia nodded, only half listening to his

words. Closing her eyes, she reached inside herself but found no lingering reminder of her servants. The only presence she felt was that of the man holding her, and just as she had told him, there was a sense of peace. For the first time since hearing her master utter the word exile, she believed she might really be okay out on her own, especially if Daniel accepted the new relationship he'd unknowingly forged.

Both of them jumped a bit as a knock landed on the dressing room door. "Hold on a minute," Daniel called out, but the door opened regardless and Valentino strolled in. If Nadia weren't fully aware of what had been done, the horrified look on his face might have been funny.

"Jesus, Val, I told you to hold on a minute."

Nadia and Valentino stared at one another while Daniel continued to curse. His words bounced off Valentino, causing no reaction whatsoever, and eventually he fell silent. Slowly, Nadia disengaged herself and stood to face Valentino's poorly restrained wrath. She smoothed her dress down, wishing it could be that easy to smooth out the current situation, but the blood on Daniel's mouth screamed her guilt.

"What did you do, Nadia?" Valentino's voice was eerily calm, but his brown eyes flashed a warning.

"We had sex, Val." Daniel stood at her side and answered before she could. The towel brushed her hip as he once more secured it at his waist. "I'd think that would be obvious."

Valentino's gaze moved slowly to Daniel. "You have blood on your lips. Is it hers?"

"Yeah, so?"

Nadia glanced at Daniel as he licked the stains away. He winked at her, and it was all she could do to force a smile while praying he would be able to forgive her.

"Nadia." Valentino hissed her name, pulling her attention back to his fierce expression. "I told you to leave him alone."

Daniel stepped in front of her. "You aren't my dad, Val, so back off."

Nadia curled her hand around Daniel's bicep and eased him back to her side. She shook her head when his gaze met hers. "It's okay, let me talk to Valentino while you take that shower you mentioned."

He shook her hand off and shot a dark look toward his boss. "What I do when I'm off the clock and who I do it with are none of your business."

"I'm trying to protect you, Danny."

"From her?" Daniel snorted. "A bit hypocritical of you, isn't it? Or have you had a change of lifestyle since I saw you last?"

"Daniel," Nadia began but neither man spared her a glance. Great. Now they were going to fight over who had the right to control her. As if either of them had any say in what she could or could not do. Were all men fools?

Valentino shook his head. "She isn't like Sera and me."

Ooh, that stung, regardless of it being true.

"You don't need to protect me from her, Val."

"As if you have any idea what she's capable of." Valentino gestured toward her. "Do you realize what she's done? Did you take her blood willingly or did she force you to drink?"

This was not how Nadia wanted Daniel to find out about their bond, but he replied before she could put a halt to the conversation.

"You really believe she could force me to do anything?"

Valentino laughed and shook his head. "Saying that just shows how naive you are."

Daniel's gaze hardened. "Is it so fucking hard for you to understand why I might want her? Why having sex with her or taking her blood, or whatever else we fucking decide to do, might be exactly what I want?"

"Calm down," Valentino murmured before glancing at Nadia. "You and I need to talk privately unless this is how you want everything to be aired."

"Don't you fucking tell me to calm down." Daniel started toward Valentino, but Nadia leapt in front of him. The look he gave her was not pleasant.

"Stop it. Let it go, okay." She laid her hand over his pounding heart.

"He's being an ass, or did you miss all that?" Daniel gestured toward Valentino but settled his angry gaze on Nadia. "Move."

"I might be an ass, but I'm also your boss."

Daniel's attention fixed over Nadia's shoulder. "So fire me because I'd like to see the paperwork on that." He shoved Nadia aside to take a menacing step toward Valentino. She could only shake her head. Adorable fool. Didn't he realize Valentino could rip him to shreds? Perhaps if they were both mortal, it would be a fair fight, but well...they weren't.

"Reason for termination: Daniel Rebiero fucked a vampire. Not sure how you'd explain that one, Val."

"You've made your point, Daniel, but it doesn't change the fact you have no idea what's happened here."

"So tell me. I can tell you're dying to." He crossed his arms and arched a brow. "Since you assume I have no idea."

Nadia narrowed her eyes and studied Daniel's face. Hmm. Maybe he knew exactly what had happened.

"It's not my place to tell you." Valentino settled another hostile gaze on Nadia. "Now, can we please have that private conversation?"

"I suppose that's up to Daniel." She glanced at him. "Well?"

"How sweet of you to ask permission, Nadia." Valentino's tone oozed sarcasm. "It isn't like you at all, does he realize that?"

Nadia ignored Valentino. "If you'd like, I'll just tell him to go to hell." What a pleasure that would be.

Daniel fixed his gaze on Valentino. "She is not to blame for what happened, just keep that in mind. You might think I'm some young, naive idiot, but I assure you the pleasure of her wrist at my mouth was one I was very aware of."

Well, that answers that.

Daniel looked at her. "Go, have your talk. I'll be here when you're through." Before she could do anything, he grabbed her and kissed her hard. Maybe it was a show for Valentino, but maybe not. The amount of emotion poured into that kiss was quite staggering, and she clung to his shoulders, returning it tenfold.

More and more, she was convinced Daniel was exactly what she needed. Perhaps being exiled was Fate's way of kicking her in the right direction? After all, she did tend to be a bit stubborn.

"Nadia." Valentino's voice ended the kiss.

"I can handle him, don't worry." She whispered against Daniel's lips then slid out of his arms. He winked to send her on her way, but despite the gesture, there was still anger in his eyes as they focused on Valentino.

"If she's not back in ten minutes, I'll come get her, and you won't like that."

Chapter Seven

"Damn you, Nadia!" Valentino slammed the office door and rounded on Nadia. After Daniel's threat, he'd all but dragged her out of the dressing room, and her arm still stung from his bruising grip. "I told you to leave my guys alone, and not only did you disobey me—"

"Whoa." Nadia held up her hand and wagged a finger. "No, no, no. You are not someone I have to obey, let's get that straight right here and now."

"When it comes to how you behave around my guys, yeah, you do have to listen to me." Sighing loudly, Valentino raked his hair off his forehead then shook it back into his eyes before turning his back to pace away from her. "Do you really think he understands what you did?"

"Do you even know what I did? You and Sera don't keep servants, and to my knowledge she never did, even while at the coven. So, the way I see it, you are assuming you know what happened and you—"

Valentino shot a glare over his shoulder. "Unless he stained his lips with his own blood, and we both know that is not the case, he is now you're servant, isn't he?"

She considered lying but decided it wouldn't change anything, and Valentino would likely sniff it out anyway. "Yes."

"Damn you, Nadia!"

"You've already said that." Crossing her arms, she leaned back against the door. A song throbbed over the loud speakers, but it couldn't drain out the high-pitched squeals of feminine delight as another gorgeous man no doubt gyrated on the stage. As long as it wasn't Daniel up there...whoa, this was no time for jealousy to intrude.

Valentino approached and stared hard at her face. "What's that look for? If either of us should be frowning, it's me."

Nadia shrugged. Valentino didn't deserve to know what might lie inside her heart, since he clearly doubted she possessed one.

"So what do you plan to do?" He asked the question as if the answer would solve all of their problems. If she needed any proof he was clueless about the vampire/servant bond, she now had it.

"I suppose I should tell Daniel what occurred, and what it means for him."

Valentino stepped back enough to cross his arms. He hadn't stopped glaring at her yet, and the look was getting old. "And if Danny wishes not to be your servant? You'll release him?"

"It's not that easy, and you wouldn't even suggest such a thing if you were a real vampire."

The glare hardened. "Maybe I'm the future of vampires, ever consider that? It's a bit old fashioned to rely on a good vein, isn't it?"

"Spoken like someone who has never had a good vein." A thought struck, and she peered hard at Valentino. "Do you feed from Sera? Or allow her to bite you?" Nadia raked her gaze down the superb length of his leather-clad body. "If so, I bet she loves every second of having her fangs deep inside—"

Valentino slammed a palm into the door close to her ear. She tried not to flinch but failed. "This is not about my relationship with Sera." He leaned close, and she expected him to growl. It'd be damn sexy if he did, but he didn't. Instead, he simply glared through the sable curtain hanging over his left eye. "Swear on whatever honor you possess, you'll give Danny a choice about all this and accept his wishes."

How dare he insinuate she had no honor? A good shove to the chest sent him stumbling away.

Irritated by what she'd accidentally done to Daniel and so over Valentino's interrogation, she shot him one of her own lethal glares. "You can go to hell, Valentino, because I won't promise you a damn thing." Before he could stop her, she spun around, yanked open the door and willed herself back to Daniel's dressing room. Valentino's harsh curse followed her the entire way.

Well, the hell with him and his demanding threats. She did not need him to point out what had been done. Did he think she could ignore the feeling of peace flowing through her veins or the awareness that only came with being bound to a mortal?

Even now, as she materialized in the center of Daniel's dressing room, his heartbeat was loud and strong in her ears and she could "feel" his presence saturating the room. Her presence called to him as well, and he seemed a bit startled when he stepped out of the bathroom. The expression quickly changed to relief after he looked her up and down and clearly found her in the same condition she'd left in.

"I'm fine, as promised."

Smiling slightly, Daniel strolled into the room, back to looking like the adorably sexy surfer she'd seduced on the beach. His damp hair hung over his forehead in dark blond waves, and the towel had been replaced by a black tank top and the camouflage shorts she'd found in his duffel bag.

"Is everything okay?"

"Of course. Valentino and I just don't see eye to eye on some things. Well, on anything, to be honest. He does not approve of the way I live my life, nor I his, so..." She shrugged. "But I'm fine, and you said you were hungry."

"Starving actually." He frowned a little while closing the distance between them. "Being with you seems to have increased my normally large appetite. Not that I'm complaining." He hugged her and planted a lingering kiss on her mouth. "I'm hungry for more than food."

Yes, his body craved things now the way hers did, only he did not realize that yet. If she were to bleed for him, he'd likely lose control, and the sooner she explained things, the better. The task was beyond daunting. What if he demanded she release him? Would she be able to honor her promise to Valentino?

Daniel was the perfect servant. Not only was he sexy, delicious and young, he made her feel safe, and not since the master had carried her into the coven had she felt so secure and protected.

Gracious, had she just compared Daniel to her master and not found him wanting? The prospect was so distracting she almost missed the shift in Daniel's embrace as it went from comforting to heated. He backed her against the wall, kissing her the entire time, and plucked at the hem of her dress. Bunching it at her waist, he kissed a hot path down her neck and paused with his mouth buried at the base of her throat. His hot, uneven breaths made her shiver.

"My God, maybe we should fuck first, eat later." Moaning, he ground his hips into her pelvis, letting her feel the erection straining his shorts. "Is it vampire tricks making me want you this bad?" His eyes were bright with lust as they met hers.

"Not exactly." He frowned, and she reached

up to play with his tousled bangs. "There is something you need to know."

"Uh-oh." Releasing her, he stepped back and took a moment to adjust the front of his shorts. "Those words never lead to anything a guy wants to hear."

"Well, that may be, but you certainly do not have to worry about me saying I am pregnant." She meant to lighten the mood, but Daniel didn't even smirk. Okay then, best to just get it over with. "Obviously you realize you consumed my blood."

His frown deepened. "Um, yeah. Hard to miss that fact when someone's bleeding wrist is pressed to your mouth."

Nadia sighed. "This will be easier if you refrain from being sarcastic."

"Sorry. Go on, I'm listening." He crossed his arms, looking very impatient and a bit angry.

Oh dear, she had a very bad feeling about all of this.

****

Nadia visibly squirmed, obviously uncomfortable, and Daniel was tempted to put her out of her misery. He already knew what she had to tell him, thanks to his very thorough questioning of Valentino once he'd discovered his boss's little secret. Turned out only two things could result from consuming vampire blood, either the drinker became a vampire or they were bound to the vampire they'd had the drink from.

Daniel was fairly certain he was not a vampire, which meant Nadia was trying to think of a way to break the news to him that he was now her servant. He waited to hear the words while she nibbled her bottom lip and fretted hard enough to wrinkle her forehead.

"There is no easy way to say this," she finally burst out. "Drinking my blood, after I've consumed yours, and while you and I were having sex, has formed a bond between us." She moistened her lips, flicked her gaze away from his and dragged her ponytail over her shoulder to toy with a few strands of blood-red hair. "I don't expect you to understand what that means."

"So tell me." But he knew. Or at least he knew some of what it meant. It meant his blood was what would sustain her, that he'd be the one keeping her "alive." As heavy as that responsibility sounded, the idea thrilled him.

When was the last time anyone had ever really needed him? Yes, hundreds of women wanted him night after night, but none of them needed him, and they quickly forgot him as soon as another guy took to the stage. But here was Nadia, a rare beautiful creature now dependent upon his blood, and she looked as though she feared the idea might disgust him.

Her gaze resettled on his face. "Do you feel any different?"

He thought about it for a moment then shrugged. "Not really. I feel tired, hungry and horny like I do most nights when it's time to go home."

"But are those feelings intensified?"

"Yeah, I guess they are." Actually, the more he thought about it, the more intense each feeling became. Mild hunger turned to gnawing stomach cramps, his cock filled with enough blood to make it achingly hard while the rest of his body longed for a nice long sleep. Staring at Nadia didn't help matters either. He wished there was a way to eat her while fucking her in his bed.

Smiling at the thought, he dropped his gaze to her neck. If she had a pulse, he couldn't see it beating under the ivory swath of skin covering her throat, and yet he knew there was blood in her veins. Good blood. Delicious blood. Blood he very much wanted to taste again.

Jesus, maybe he was wrong and he was a vampire?

"No, you most definitely are not a vampire."

He jerked his attention to her face. "Did you just read my mind?"

She nodded. "It's invasive to do so, so forgive me."

"But if you can read my mind, then you know I know."

"No, I read only the one thought, just now." She hesitated and narrowed her eyes. "What exactly do you know?"

He quickly cleared his thoughts of anything Valentino might have told him in the past.

"Nothing, go on with what you were saying. The bond we forged and all that."

Waving her hand in the air, she sighed. "It's a long, boring explanation, so I'll just get right to the point. You are my servant now, and I suppose if you wish not to be, I'll release you."

Hearing the words out loud sent an unexpected shock through him. When he'd gotten out of bed this morning, his only goal had been to enjoy the sun and waves before he had to come to work. He had not anticipated seeing Nadia again or anything that followed, but here he was faced with a rather staggering decision to make. To be or not be Nadia's servant.

If he wished it, she'd release him, or so she claimed. Hadn't Valentino told him about the possessive streak in vampires? Would Nadia really let him go if he asked her to? He wasn't too sure he even wanted to find out. There had to be worse twists of fate than to find yourself bound to a sexy vampire. In fact, it actually seemed kind of cool.

"Cool?" Nadia's eyes widened. "Did you really just conclude that this is cool?"

"I thought you said reading minds is invasive?"

"Some thoughts are too astounding to ignore. Now answer me. Did I read you correctly?"

"Yes, I guess I did." He couldn't help but chuckle as her expression turned even more incredulous. "That surprises you, I take it?"

"You don't have a thousand questions? You aren't the least bit afraid of what it might mean for you? You're just going to accept it?"

"Right now? Yeah, I'm just going to accept it." He laughed at her irritated expression and grabbed her hand to pull her away from the wall. "Sorry if you were hoping for a fight, and maybe after I eat I'll have the energy to give you one, but not right now. Let me process all this over a hot meal then let me take you to bed and then maybe, just maybe I'll freak out. Sound good, mistress?"

"You don't have to call me that."

He tipped her chin up and swept his thumb over her bottom lip. "No, but you like it, don't you?" Moving his finger, he sucked her lip into his mouth and sipped at her. "Later, I'll get on my knees and call you that."

Reaching up, she shoved her hands through his hair and pulled his face back with shocking force. Her eyes were the color of wet slate. "Why not do it now?"

"Because I really am hungry." But, God, he wanted her.

"So eat me, and if you're a good boy, I'll give you more blood." She released him and took a few steps back to lean against the wall. Holding his gaze, she lifted her dress to her waist, exposing pale thighs and a tempting little strip of blood-red hair. "And don't forget to call me mistress while on your knees."

Daniel's mouth went dry, and all thought of

real food flew out the window. Dropping to his knees, he gripped Nadia's slender hips and buried his face between her legs. She smelled intoxicatingly good, a musky mixture of sex, woman and, he assumed, vampire.

Holding her in place, he parted her folds with his tongue, causing her to squeak and tug at his hair while pushing her hips closer to his face. By feel, he found her opening and plunged his tongue inside.

"Oh my God." She arched toward him and slung a leg over his shoulder, opening herself wider and allowing his tongue to go deeper. In no time, his mouth burned with her taste and her juices saturated his chin. He rubbed his face against her pussy, wanting to coat every inch of skin he could. Shuddering in response, she begged him to let her come.

Daniel dragged his tongue along her clit then sat on his heels to look up. "Your wish is my command, mistress. Just tell me how to please you."

"Oh God." Closing her eyes, she dropped her chin to her chest. "For God's sake, just do it."

Instead of moving toward her, he pulled her hips away from the wall until his face was between her legs again, then he began to lick her in long, even strokes. Her wet curls teased his lips, her smell filled his senses and her taste nearly drove him mad. By the time she climaxed with a soft cry of pleasure, his shorts had grown way too tight over his erection, and his balls ached with a fierce pain that demanded release.

Barely letting her finish the orgasmic ride, he pulled her down to the floor, shoved her onto her back and ripped open his shorts. His cock peeked from the top of his underwear, ready to be freed.

While Nadia gasped softly and struggled to open her eyes, he spread her legs and drove inside her. Her passage still throbbed from the recent orgasm and the muscles tightened, sucking him deep. The pleasure was unlike anything he'd ever felt. Holding still to ward off the climax he could feel building, he focused on her face. She turned to graze his wrist with her teeth, making him lose a little bit of the control already slipping away.

"Yeah, go ahead," he panted, while forcing his cock as far as it would go. "Let me feel those fangs of yours."

Nadia parted her beautiful lips and bit him. The subtle pain couldn't compete with the ache in his balls, and his release raced closer and closer as she sucked at his arm. If there was any sight sexier than her ruby lips parted over his tanned skin, damned if he knew what it might be.

After a few moments, her bite weakened, and a drop of blood rolled toward the floor. Watching her tongue trail after it was all it took to end his quest for pleasure.

The intensity of his orgasm almost made him howl, and it seemed to take forever to be able to breathe again. When he could, he collapsed at Nadia's side with his arm still draped across her chest. Wearing a blissful expression, she continued to feed, and a heavy awareness blossomed in his heart. Fuck, he was in love.

"That was unbelievable." Those three words were easier to form than the other three hovering on his tongue.

"Mmm," she murmured against his skin. After a few more drags from his vein, she slid her fangs free and rolled her head around to look at him. Her eyes were a bright, clear shade of silver, and it wouldn't be hard at all to spend the rest of forever staring into them.

A smile touched her lips. "I didn't make you a vampire, my darling."

Daniel rolled the rest of the way off Nadia and propped his head on his hand. "Are there any perks at all to becoming your servant?" There had to be more than mind blowing sex and the exchange of blood.

"Several." Her smile grew, and she reached over to press a finger to his lips. "But we'll discuss all of that while you eat. I've taken a great deal of blood from you tonight, and doing so weakens you. We can't have that, can we?"

As if on cue, his stomach growled. "I'm outnumbered, it seems." After landing a quick kiss on her soft lips, he jumped to his feet and fixed his clothes. "You'll tell me how you know Valentino, too, right? Or do all vampires just know each other? Did you share a, what would it be, coven?"

"Does all that matter?"

Daniel finished fastening his shorts and turned to Nadia. She caught his eye while smoothing the hem of her dress into place. "Yeah," he told her. "It matters. I want to know everything about you."

Her expression closed just a little. "Even the unpleasant stuff?"

"Especially the unpleasant stuff."

She rolled her eyes. "Leave it to me to find another rebellious servant."

Daniel grabbed his duffel bag and motioned for Nadia to precede him to the door. When she was at his side, he grabbed her hand and turned her to face him. "You'll explain that remark as well."

With ease, she slid free of his grasp and flashed a hard to read smile. "Perhaps."

Chapter Eight

Nadia tried not to grimace as Daniel took an enormous bite of his hamburger. Ketchup and mustard dripped out onto his fries, not that he seemed to care. Smiling, he shoved a few fries into his mouth, chewed and swallowed. At the moment it didn't matter how adorable he was, she had to look away.

"So, is that the whole story?" Ice clinked in Daniel's glass, telling her it was safe to look.

"Is that not enough?" She'd told him about her exile, she'd told him about having to part ways with the coven so what else was there to tell? Seemed enough to her, minus a few details, but what he didn't know wouldn't hurt him.

Daniel put the burger down and shrugged. "Just seems like there should be more. Why were you exiled? I mean, yeah, you pissed off the master, but why?"

"I guess he was having a bad day and I was the desired target."

"Yeah, don't buy that, sweetheart. Try again." He watched her while eating more fries.

Nadia glared at the food. "That looks truly disgusting."

"This?" Daniel waved a fry in the air, making it flop in half. "Don't tell me you never ate a French fry?"

"I am very relieved to say that I have not."

His brows lowered. "How old are you? I mean, how long have you been a vampire?" His voice dropped around the last word, and he glanced around.

"One hundred years, and it is impolite for a man to ask any woman her age." She arched a brow, but he laughed.

"There weren't fries one hundred years ago? What a pity." He ate the floppy fry. "But anyway, why did the master target you?"

Oh, did it really prove anything to keep all this to herself? "His wife felt threatened by me." Daniel's mouth formed a perfect O, but he said nothing. Clearly she was supposed to elaborate. "Can you blame her?"

"Nope." The quickness of his reply thrilled her. "Any woman would feel threatened by you, you're more than gorgeous."

"And you are a divine flatterer." Nadia reached across the table to grab his hand. "Will you understand if I say this subject is difficult for me to discuss?" She stroked his wrist, feeling the pulse increase with each brush of her fingers.

"I just want to understand you, Nadia, because I don't think a lot of people really do."

She pulled back and crossed her arms. "Why would you say that?" Mortal insight always bothered her.

"Let's use Valentino as an exam—"

"Must we?"

Daniel chuckled. "He obviously thinks you're some violent creature determined to hurt—"

"He thinks that way about all real vampires."

"Stop interrupting." She snapped her mouth shut, and he continued. "But he's wrong, and we both know it. I doubt you'd hurt anyone, for any reason."

"God, do not delude yourself by thinking I'm harmless. I could give you an example of how dangerous I can be, if you'd like?" She glanced around the moderately crowded restaurant and zeroed in on a lovely blonde sipping a glass of water.

"Nadia, don't."

Narrowing her eyes, she focused on the glass. "But it'll be fun." Her voice dropped to a husky whisper as her power built. "Just watch." Daniel slapped his palm on their table, jerking her gaze toward him and breaking her concentration. "Why did you do that?"

"My point is, Valentino is wrong about you, and I'm sure he isn't the only one."

"Maybe I am trying very hard to show you a different side of myself? Ever think of that?" She leaned over the table, catching his hand again. "I want you to like me, or you will make a very horrible servant."

"Speaking of servants. Did you have one at

the coven?"

"Of course I did, and it made leaving even more difficult. Not that the master cared one whit about any of that."

"Does he hope this exile will kill you?" There was a dark anger lying beneath the question, and Daniel's fingers flexed under her hand. "Were you supposed to starve to death or something?"

"I do not think that is possible, actually. Though it would be horrible to be denied blood for too long."

"Just tell me if that's what he wanted." His voice lacked the lightness she had forced into her tone.

"I have no idea what he hopes for, to be honest. My presence was no longer desired within the coven, so he threw me out." She shrugged, hating how trivial it all sounded. "Be assured, however, that I have no desire to die, and now that I have you, I know I will survive and then some."

"I'll give you whatever you need for however long you want it."

Hearing those words was worth watching Daniel eat all the disgusting fries he wished to.

"Thank you." Odd that the words *I love you* actually hovered on her tongue.

****

Daniel knew there was more, much more, to Nadia's story than she'd shared, but he also wasn't stupid enough to push. In time, she'd tell him everything he needed to know, and he'd be right by her side when that time came if she agreed to his plan.

"Move in with me." Her eyes widened in shock at his suggestion, the silvery color reflecting the florescent lights above them. "Come on," he went on before she could say anything. "You know it makes sense. Shouldn't a vampire be with their servant?"

"Yes."

"Well then, enough said." Suddenly anxious to take her home, he pushed the rest of his food away and signaled for the check. "You'll probably hate my place, but you can make any changes you want to."

"Daniel—"

"It's not a dump, at least, but it certainly lacks a feminine touch."

"Daniel—"

"Though I'm not sure where we'll put your coffin." He winked and she scowled. "Kidding. Val told me most of the crap written about you guys is wrong."

"Yes." Her voice sounded tight.

The waitress slapped the check on the table and waited for Daniel to hand over the money. "Just take the tip out of that." She nodded and left without glancing in Nadia's direction.

"Would it kill her to be polite?"

"You are rather intimidating, Nadia. Can't blame the girl." He grabbed her hand and tugged her to her feet. "Let's go home."

"Daniel—"

He silenced her with a kiss. At first she was rigid and unresponsive, and he knew it had nothing to do with the fact that they were in the middle of a restaurant. Wrapping his arms around her, he pulled her closer, forced her lips apart and thrust his tongue inside. She moaned and melted. After a few more seconds, he pulled back but didn't let her go.

"Stop trying to protest, because no matter what you say, you are moving in with me."

"I do not like being told what to do." She licked her lips and dropped her gaze to his. If ever a woman looked like they wanted another kiss, it was Nadia at that precise moment.

"Well, after this I won't do it often."

"What if I don't want to move in with you?"

Daniel shrugged and lowered his face until his lips barely touched hers. "You should have thought of that before you fed me your delicious blood." She sucked in a sharp breath as he pulled back without kissing her. "Now, let's go home."

Her glare all but burned a hole in his back, but he didn't care. He felt like he'd just won the shiniest trophy imaginable.

Nadia was his, and he was hers. Life was good.

****

Life wasn't so good a week later as Daniel checked his reflection in the mirror one more time. His hair refused to cooperate, probably because he should have trimmed it days ago. But with Nadia moving in and taking over, personal grooming ceased to be a priority. Too bad all the product he'd gooped on wasn't working. Oh well, he doubted the women would care once the music started and his clothes came off.

Tossing his head upside down, he raked his fingers through the stubborn hair then took another look. The wild, just out of bed look should earn him some extra money. A knock at the door signaled the end to his primping.

"Yeah, I need one more second," he called.

"You still have some time before your set."

Daniel turned from the mirror as Valentino stepped into the room and closed the door. This didn't bode well. "What's up, Val?"

Valentino looked around the small dressing room and began to scowl. "Is she here?"

"Who?" Fuck, he sounded guilty.

"Nadia. Is she here?" Valentino's gaze was cold and steady when it settled on Daniel. "And please don't lie."

"Why would you ask that?" Daniel gestured around the room. "And do you see her?"

"I smell her."

Uh oh. "Excuse me?"

"Her unique aroma is all over you, like you've rolled around on top of her, but that would be really stupid wouldn't it?"

Daniel swallowed. "Why would that be stupid?"

"I told you to stay away from her, didn't I? And here you are reeking of her." Val shook his head and leaned back against the door. "I won't tolerate her presence, Danny. Nor are my feelings open for discussion."

"Yeah, well guess what, Val? My feelings aren't open for discussion either. Now if you'll excuse me." He pushed away from the vanity and stalked toward the door. "I think I have to go out there and make you some money."

Valentino grabbed Daniel's arm and applied enough pressure to make him worry about bruises. "If you don't get rid of her, you will be looking for new employment."

"I'm getting tired of that threat. Either fire me now or fuck off." Daniel ripped his arm free and managed to get the door open. He should have known though that Val would manage to get the last word.

"I could just wait until she shows her true nature and then say I told you so. It's up to you, Danny, but you've been warned."

"Whatever," Daniel mumbled on his way out the door. Fuck Valentino and his "warnings." The guy was dead wrong about Nadia, and what the hell could he possibly know about her true nature? If it weren't for the creepy way Val and his girl, Sera, were dedicated to one another, Daniel would assume this all stemmed from jealousy. But obviously, Val just hated Nadia for the sake of hating her. Well, too fucking bad.

"Hey, Danny boy." Dominic, a fellow dancer

and all around nosy guy, loped up. "How's it feel to have a chic living with you? Has she tossed out all your shit yet?"

The air behind Daniel turned to ice, but somehow he ignored it. "It's not that bad, Dom. You should try it."

Dominic snorted. "Sure, when I'm fifty. How's that sound?" His gaze slid past Daniel. "Hey, Val. What the fuck has you looking so pissed? The place is packed, the women are horny as hell and the money is literally flying out of their hands." He patted his six pack, freshly coated with sweat from his recent turn on stage. "I'd like to think I have something to do with all that good news."

"I need to speak to Daniel, Dominic." Val's tone matched the chill in the air.

Dominic shivered and arched a brow at Daniel. "Wouldn't want to be you, buddy. Good luck." He walked away, humming the melody of the song playing in the club.

"She is living with you?"

Daniel turned slowly. "Yes."

Wow, that one word cost a great deal. The chill in Valentino's eyes worsened until they no longer looked brown but more solid, unrelenting black. Fuck. Maybe it was a good thing that Val didn't feed off mortals because if he looked at them the way he was looking at Daniel, they'd die before he even managed to get his fangs close.

"You actually allowed that...creature to

move in with you?"

"Creature, eh?" Daniel's anger easily replaced any unease. "Correct me if I'm wrong, but wasn't your precious Sera the same sort of creature when you two met?" Shit, he'd gone too far.

Val exploded, and in a flash, had Daniel pinned to the wall with a cruel hand in the center of his chest. "Just think about this. Everything I can do, Nadia can do probably one hundred times better." He applied more pressure to Daniel's chest. "Are you really sure that's what you want to sleep next to? Are you really that sure you can handle her?"

Had he been able to breathe, he might have responded.

Val leaned closer, and the pressure to Daniel's chest increased. "I could snap your ribs right now without a great deal of effort, and yet, Nadia could push them straight through to the other side."

"I get it," Daniel managed to rasp.

Val eased up. "Get rid of her, for your own good."

"I can't." Daniel rubbed his chest, praying to God Val hadn't left a hand print through the thin T-shirt.

"You must."

"Jesus, Val, I can't. Don't you get it? I can't." Just the thought of going home to an empty place sent a chill down his spine. Nadia hadn't just moved into his house, she'd moved into his being. He liked that Val could smell her on him. He liked it a lot.

"If you think the bond is unbreakable—"

"Fuck the bond," Daniel interrupted. "Even without that, I'd want her. And before you tell me I'll grow bored and toss her aside like all the other chics, forget that. You're wrong. She's different, and not because she's a vampire."

"She has you under some sort of spell."

Daniel chuckled, and it hurt. Shit. "She isn't a witch, Val. She's a vampire. And she needs me."

Now it was Valentino's turn to laugh. "Nadia needs no one but herself."

"You're wrong, and I won't leave her." They stared at one another for a long time. Finally, Valentino sighed.

"If I see her around the club, both of you will be sorry." It was a small victory, but Daniel would take it. Hopefully Nadia would accept it as well.

Chapter Nine

There was something wrong with the placement of the furniture, but Nadia couldn't figure out what. In her mind everything had looked just right, but once the old stuff had been moved out to make room for the new, nothing had fallen into place the way she'd envisioned. Maybe Daniel would know what was wrong.

Glancing at the clock—the new clock she'd hung over a new desk—she ticked the hours off in her head until he would return home. Time had never mattered so much to her at the coven, but here, it seemed to be all that mattered. Odd how two hours could feel like an eternity.

With a loud sigh, she threw herself across the new spacious sectional just as the door opened and Daniel walked in. She perked up instantly. "What are you doing home?"

He tossed his keys aside, along with his sweatjacket and headed for her without even noticing the new furniture. The energy around him radiated irritation and anxiety, and her first thought was that he'd lost his job.

Nadia sat up a little straighter. "What has happened?"

"Valentino." It was all Daniel said before he grabbed her hands, pulled her to her feet and kissed her. There was a scorching need to the embrace impossible to ignore, and Nadia gladly clung to Daniel's shoulders to kiss him back with all she was worth.

"I need you," he murmured against her lips.

"Yes, all right." As if she would say no.

Daniel pulled back, shaking his head. "No. I need you. All of you. Not just sex."

Good Lord, what exactly was he asking her to give? The past week had been blissfully wonderful, but if he expected her to hand over the small bit that even Jason and Chase had never possessed, it was much too soon.

"I—" Another kiss silenced her, but it lasted only long enough to make her crave another.

"I need this bond between us reaffirmed. Can you do that for me?"

Ah, so that was it. He was having doubts about her, and she knew very well Valentino had put them there. She was very curious as to what had been said, but she'd ask later. Daniel looked too on edge for her to ignore his request.

"Yes. I can do whatever you want or need me to do." She stroked his cheek, feeling just a hint of the stubble he removed every morning. "You have no reason to doubt our bond, Daniel."

He shook his head then snatched her hand from his cheek. "It's not you I doubt, okay?"

"No, it is never okay if I do not understand what is going on." Slipping from his arms, she put some space between them. "You are having doubts about your feelings for me? Is that what you mean?"

Daniel shrugged and raked his hair off his forehead. "I don't know. I don't think so, but Val thinks this is all based on some sort of spell or something."

Nadia snickered. "I am not a witch, and he knows that."

"I know, and I said exactly the same thing when he suggested you had put some sort of spell on me." He sighed and dropped onto the sectional, pulling her down beside him. "I don't know. I just don't know. He's so against us being together, and he flipped out when Dom let it slip that you had moved in. Jesus, I've never seen his eyes so cold and scary."

"Did he fire you?"

"No, but I've been warned." He rubbed his chest and winced. "It was a warning I won't forget either, and if you show up at the club, I will be fired."

"He is such an ass."

Daniel laughed and wrapped his arms around her. "He's actually not, but you seem to turn him into one."

"I've always had a strange affect on men."

"Oh?" Daniel eased back and tilted her face up. "Speaking of, I mean what I said. I want to strengthen the bond between us, if that's possible."

"It is very possible, but are you sure?"

"Yeah, I'm sure." He spread his fingers against her throat and stroked the underside of her chin with his thumb. "Just tell me how."

Nadia swallowed as her body began to react to Daniel's touch. "It is all about the blood. The more you take the more bound you are to me."

His fingers slid around to her nape to pull her closer. "Then feed me." The words feathered over her cheek then he pressed a soft kiss close to her ear. "Feed me while I fuck you."

Nadia sucked in a sharp breath. "Yes."

Daniel eased her back and reached for the buttons of her blouse. He held her gaze while undoing the shirt and spreading it open to expose her bra. Even when he cupped her breasts, he didn't look away from her eyes, and Nadia doubted she possessed the strength to shift her attention elsewhere either. Arching into his hands, she pressed her hard nipples against his palms.

"Touch me," she begged.

Dragging the bra out of the way, he pinched her nipples, causing a shock of painful pleasure to race through her. She gasped, and he released the sensitive tips to scoop the weight of her breasts into his hands. He shoved them together and leaned over her until his face was almost too close to focus on. The nearness of his lips was too much to bear, but she couldn't reach them, not with his hands kneading her breasts and pinning her to the sofa.

"Take your clothes off." As rebellious as

Jason could be, never would he have given such an order.

"Are you going to say please?"

Daniel shook his head instead of answering and squeezed her breasts a little tighter.

Nadia closed her eyes and absorbed the pleasure of his touch. "I cannot take off my clothes with you on top of me."

Before she could reopen her eyes, he released her. The imprint of his touch lingered on her breasts, and she covered the tingling spots with her own hands and squeezed.

Daniel hissed, and she opened her eyes to see him standing over her. The look on his face was priceless. She watched him watch her hands skim down her body toward the top of her jeans. A muscle ticked in his jaw when she undid the buttons, and his nostrils flared as she arched off the sectional to push the denim past her hips.

"Nadia."

Smiling at the rough desire in his tone, she kicked the jeans off and threw them on the floor. "Yes, my darling?"

He parted his lips, but nothing came out as she laid her hand at the juncture of her thighs. The lace panties she wore shredded under her nails, allowing her to bury her fingers between her legs. Seeking the slick warmth of her opening, she arched her hips again, dropped her knees open and slid one finger deep inside.

Daniel fell to his knees and gripped her

thigh hard. He pushed her leg higher, exposing her more fully to his wild gaze. Licking his lips, he lowered his face close to her pussy. She began to slip her finger free, but he grabbed her wrist to stop her.

"No." His breath was close enough to make her clitoris swell. "Finger-fuck yourself while I eat you." He moved her wrist, sliding her finger in and out until she took over. "Yes, like that." This time, when he spoke, his lips brushed her flesh then he snaked his tongue out for a long, thorough lick.

Nadia shoved her finger as deep as it would go then added another one. All the while, Daniel licked and sucked at her clitoris. As good as it felt, she still recalled the need he had voiced. He wanted more blood, and she wanted to give it to him flavored with the spice of her orgasm. Lifting her free hand to her mouth, she tore open her wrist and coaxed the blood to the surface.

"Daniel, my darling." He looked up without taking his mouth from her, and his gaze fixed on the blood dripping down her forearm. His eyes widened with hunger. "You have to come get it."

She dropped her hand above her head, letting it dangle over the arm of the sofa. It didn't matter if blood dripped on the new rug she'd placed over the wood floor. Nothing mattered as Daniel pushed to his feet then straddled her chest. He reached for her arm, but she shook her head.

"No. You cannot have it yet."

He dropped his gaze to her face. "You'll stop bleeding if I wait much longer."

"Your impatience is incredibly appealing, have I ever told you that?" Before he could answer, she nodded toward his shorts. "Undo those."

With no hesitation, he ripped open his shorts and dragged his hard cock out, stroking it until it stood nice and tall. Moisture dripped from the tip, catching Nadia's full attention.

"Is this what you want?" His tone oozed arrogance. "You want to suck me while I suck at your wrist?" He scooted closer and ran the tip of his cock along her mouth. "Hmm? Go ahead, open up."

Nadia parted her lips, and Daniel thrust inside. Moaning, she did nothing to stop him as he reached for her arm and sealed his mouth to her wrist. He wasn't able to thrust and drink at the same time, not that it mattered. The weight of his thick cock on her tongue was pleasurable enough, and she happily sucked and licked at the fat head.

More moisture beaded at the tip to reward her for her efforts, and as she swallowed it down, she began to move her fingers inside her sex once more. Her muscles already quivered with an inevitable orgasm, and she knew it wouldn't be long. Would Daniel notice the difference in the taste of her blood?

A moan rumbled out of him, and the

pressure at her wrist increased. He nudged his cock deeper into her mouth then thrust in and out with jerky moves. She mimicked his actions with her hand, and her vaginal muscles responded by closing around her fingers. It became harder to move her hand, and finally, she gave up and simply pressed her palm over her clitoris.

At the contact, her body came undone. She screamed around Daniel's cock, which twitched, throbbed and then sprayed hot cum down her throat. When the last drop was gone, she removed her hand from between her legs and gripped Daniel's hip to push him back. His cock slid from her mouth, and he licked her wrist after one more good drag at her vein.

Shaking, he braced his hands on either side of her head and dropped his chin to his chest. "Oh, my God." He dragged in a few breaths before speaking again. "It has never tasted like that."

"So you did notice a difference."

He nodded then stretched out between her legs, still keeping his weight on his hands. After a quick kiss, he tossed his hair out of his eyes and smiled. "I don't think I want to drink from you ever again if you aren't having an orgasm."

Nadia laughed. "I think that can be arranged, but I also do not think you mean that."

He dropped his head to her shoulder then slowly lowered his weight onto her. "Am I hurting you?"

"No, I'm a bit more durable than you might think." She wrapped her arms and legs around him to hold him even closer. "Are you still having doubts?"

He shook his head against her shoulder. "No. I think I am exactly where I should be."

Nadia shifted under him until she felt the head of his cock settle at her opening. "Now you are exactly where you should be."

He hardened a little and tried to push inside. "Ugh, I can't." Lifting his head, he met her gaze. "Not yet, anyway. Give me a few minutes."

"I'm not going anywhere." She brushed his bangs out of his eyes then eased his head back down to her shoulder. In no time, he was sound asleep. Smiling at nothing in particular, Nadia buried her face in the soft strands of Daniel's hair and held him while he slept.

****

"Why are you so agreeable to this?" Nadia's voice roused Daniel.

Still a little weak, he rose onto his hands to look at her. "Agreeable to what? You?" She nodded and began to stroke her finger up and down his Adam's apple. "That's not an easy question to answer."

"Try." Something in her tone turned the moment very serious.

With a sigh, Daniel moved off Nadia then pulled her onto his lap. "I like the idea that you need me." She arched a brow but said nothing, and he struggled to find the words to further explain himself.

"There's a lot you don't know about me."

"So tell me now."

He covered her lips and smiled. "Hush and I will." Nipping his finger lightly, she nodded for him to go on. "My grand scheme in life was not to become a stripper, you know? I actually have a degree in Marine Biology, and the plan was to graduate college and head to the Amazon to join the efforts to save wildlife down—"

"But?" She interrupted despite the pressure of his fingers on her lips.

"But an ex-girlfriend convinced me to interview at Captive Fantasy and I did, and I guess as they say the rest is history, along with her."

"If you didn't like the job, you would not still be doing it."

"True. There's a certain satisfaction that comes with working a crowd into a wild frenzy, but it doesn't erase the craving I have to spend my life doing something a hell of a lot more important, you know?"

She was quiet for a few moments, simply gazing up at him with searching eyes. "Daniel?" she finally said.

"Yeah?"

"I am not exactly some unfortunate Amazon creature in need of saving."

"You sure about that?" He hugged her close

and kissed the top of her head as she tried to frown at him. "You might not be from the rainforest, but I think you do need me to save you, and I think that's a very worthy cause to focus on."

"Suit yourself." She said it with a shrug, but he heard the pleasure in her tone. He hugged her closer and tighter, ready to wait for her to admit just how thrilled she was that he was willing to stay, no matter how long that wait turned out to be.

Chapter Ten

It had been two weeks, and still Nadia could not believe she actually lived with Daniel. Several times she'd wondered what her answer would have been had he asked instead of demanded.

"You better not be plotting some horrible demise for those." Daniel came up behind her and wrapped her in a warm, delicious smelling embrace. "You might hate the beach and all things associated with it, but those cost a pretty penny."

Nadia turned her back on the six surfboards she'd been contemplating and nestled against Daniel's chest. He was on his way to work, and just like every night, she wished he would stay here with her. "I don't hate everything associated with the beach."

"Name one thing."

She glanced up. "You."

His answering smile pleased her, and she knew moving in had been the right thing to do. Now she just needed to get used to how alarmingly domesticated she'd become. The other night, she'd actually passed the time watching a cooking show. Scary, very scary. But what else was there to do?

At least among the coven, she'd had a purpose, even though it had only been to serve the master. Still, it was something. But here, with Daniel, what was her purpose? To keep the home fires burning until he got back home? God, that was so not her.

"What are you thinking about so hard?"

Nadia shook her head against his chest. "Just stuff, I guess."

"Stuff." Easing back, he held her at arm's length. "Such as?"

Dare she? One look in his hazel eyes let her know it was now or never.

"I'm bored, Daniel, and when I get bored bad things happen."

"Is that so? Do you call the fires of hell to the surface? Or maybe you go on a hunting rampage, killing without conscience—"

"Stop it, I'm being serious." She pulled away from him and turned her back. Again, she stared at the surfboards. "It is not in my nature to sit here while you go out night after night to live your life. I don't like it."

"I'd take you with me if I could."

Nadia whipped back around, seizing the very opportunity she'd hoped for. "And why can't you?"

"Other than the threat hanging over my head from Val?"

"Forget him, and besides, what's the worst

he could do to you?"

Daniel scraped his hair off his forehead and shook his head. "Other than fire me?"

"You don't need this job. You have a degree in..." She waved her hand. "What is it again?"

Daniel moved away to finish packing his duffel bag. "Marine Biology," he told her while shoving a pair of shorts inside. "And there is no way I could make what I make at the club saving Brazilian otters."

"So save something bigger and more important, or is the job more about the attention?"

His sexy chuckle bugged her at the same time it turned her on. "Maybe. I'll admit the attention, the screams, the looks of lust, all of it is like a drug, and I like the high. Do you hold that against me?"

Nadia shook her head. She couldn't judge him when she completely understood what it was like to possess such power over the desire of others. But understanding why Daniel did what he did only made her want to experience it more.

He chuckled again and pressed his lips to hers. "Stop frowning." After a quick kiss, he headed for the door.

"I'm serious, Daniel. I want to come with you tonight." She was very afraid if he told her no, her restlessness might drive them apart. They'd only been together a short time, but she knew in that part of her she rarely explored, he was someone capable of fulfilling her for as long as eternity lasted. That being said, she still needed more than fantastic blood and amazing sex. She needed to live, to feel as though she belonged with him. And that meant getting the hell out of this apartment.

Daniel shook his head. His hair was still damp from the shower, and she loved the way it feathered over the bridge of his nose. "You know you can't."

"Actually, I can, and Val need not know I'm there." For God's sake, she was a vampire, and it was high time she acted like one again.

Daniel stared at her, clearly giving it a lot of thought.

Damn, it never occurred to her that maybe he liked that she couldn't watch his performance. "Do you want me there?"

"Of course I want you there. I'd love to dance for you." His hand flexed on the doorknob. "Are you sure you can hide from Valentino?"

"Yes." She hoped so, anyway.

"Tell me, is it our bond that makes it impossible for me to say no to you, or the fact that I love you?"

The moment the words slipped out, he snapped his mouth shut and his eyes filled with a staggering array of emotions. Nadia didn't need to probe his thoughts, not in the face of such an open gaze, but she did. What she found thrilled her. He loved her, even if he hadn't been ready to say so out loud, it was true.

Who knew how many times she'd been told "I love you" by past servants, but there was something about the way Daniel had said it without really intending to that made the sentiment mean so much more. He hadn't used the words to prove his loyalty or his worth. He'd just stated a fact as if telling her the sky was still blue during the day.

Damn, if she were any weaker, she might cry. Instead, she held her tongue, despite the urge to respond in kind, and waited for Daniel to give in and tell her she could go with him.

He flashed a smile that thrilled Nadia just as much as the proclamation of love had. "Do you need to change?"

With a little squeal, she jumped at him to kiss him then flew to the bedroom to change. Just in case she couldn't hide from all eyes, she wanted to look good. Hell, she wanted to look better than any other woman there.

"You have five minutes, gorgeous," Daniel called from the living room.

Twenty minutes later, and dressed in a slinky black, toga-style dress, Nadia promised Daniel all sorts of wicked pleasures if he'd just stop worrying about being late. She took his hand, pressed her lips to his and said, "Close your eyes."

When he opened them, they were in his dressing room.

"I'll never get used to that."

Nadia laughed on her way to the bathroom

to check her hair and makeup. "Yes, you will." While she listened to Daniel changing in the other room, she pulled her hair out of its ponytail and tossed her head upside down to make the blood-red mane good and fluffy. After some artful arranging of a few stubborn strands and a good amount of hairspray, she was pleased with the result.

"You aren't supposed to be seen," Daniel commented from the doorway. "So why do you have to look so sexy?"

"Maybe I just want to look sexy so you'll say I do." Her good humor faded a bit as she took in what he was wearing, or what he wasn't wearing, depending on how one chose to view things. His lush, golden body was exposed for all the world to see save for a pair of bright red shorts. And why bother with the shorts, considering she could clearly see the outline of all he had to offer against the spandex?

Under the weight of her gaze, he stepped back and spread his arms. "What do you think?"

"I hate it." Actually, he looked damn sexy. Growing more and more irritated, she lifted her gaze to his face. "But I don't understand. You're going to strip out of those? And end up in what?"

He tugged at the waistband to expose a glimpse of the mesh g-string underneath. "Don't worry, we don't do naked."

It was the same g-string she'd seen the very first night, and he might as well be naked.

"You look jealous." He nipped her under the

chin with a finger while putting the red shorts back in order. "Maybe you should have stayed home?"

Yeah, maybe.

"I'll behave," she promised. Unless some bitch got too close, and Nadia was forced to start breaking hands and ripping eyes out. Though she could always just wipe the memory of every woman clean so they couldn't remember how yummy Daniel looked. Hmm, that possibility had merit.

A heavy knock sounded at the door, and Daniel winked at her. "That's my cue. Behave, whatever you do, okay?" He kissed her quick and headed for the door, but Nadia had other ideas.

Wrapping her hand around his arm, she pulled him to a stop and flattened him against the wall. He opened his mouth to speak, but she cupped her hand over his lips and shook her head. He narrowed his eyes but didn't fight her.

"I want to give you something before you go out there." Leaning into him, she licked the side of his neck, tasting coconut and everything else that made him so delicious.

"Careful, you don't want me going out there with a hard-on." Too late, if the pressure against her lower belly was any indication.

After another swipe of her tongue over his skin, she brought her wrist to her mouth and pierced a vein. As the blood welled to the surface, she met Daniel's gaze. "I want the taste of me in your mouth as you dance for them."

He licked his lips, fighting to keep his eyes away from her wrist. "Just because, or is there something else going on here?"

Nadia loved how intuitive he was. Nodding, she smeared the blood with her right hand then painted his lips with her stained fingers. "Every time you take my blood, it strengthens our bond, and I want to feel what you feel while you're on that stage." She shuddered with pleasure as he sucked two fingers into his mouth. "And I want you to feel what I feel."

He released her fingers with a little popping sound. "God help me."

Looking adorably eager, he grabbed her wrist and brought the wound to his mouth. Normally, he closed his eyes when he fed from her, but not now. Their gazes locked, and her blood flowed faster.

Too much blood would make their bond unbearably strong, and there was no time to satisfy the sexual need that would awaken, so she had no choice but to stop him after only a few moments.

Gently, she twisted her fingers in his hair and pulled him away from her wrist. "Enough, my darling."

His eyes sparkled as he licked his lips. "It's very cruel to offer only a small taste, mistress."

She smiled, knowing he only called her that when she was in for some truly wicked loving. "You can have all you want later. Now go before

Valentino comes looking for you and finds me instead."

"You're an evil tease."

Nadia laughed. "Yes, and yet I'm not the one flaunting my half naked body." She shoved him toward the door before he could say anything in defense. "Go, and yes, I'll behave."

And she had every intention of doing so, just as long as the other women behaved as well.

****

Nadia came to learn several things while watching performer after performer take the stage. First, each dancer danced three sets and sometimes a fourth depending on crowd reaction. Second, every woman in attendance was in desperate need of a long night of sex. And last but not least, every woman in attendance annoyed the hell out of her.

Did they have any idea how desperate and pathetic they looked, shrieking like zoo animals and waving money in the air? Clearly they believed whoever yelled the loudest and held the money the highest would convince the guys to hop off the stage to take the tip personally. Thankfully, that had yet to happen.

Utilizing a small degree of mind control, Nadia stood undetected against the back bar. She had a clear view of the stage, as well as the crowd, and she'd had about all she could take of one especially rowdy table of women. All through Daniel's first two sets they had hooted and taunted, chipping away at her patience little by little. Their behavior now, while he began his third set, was no better. She kept her eyes on them despite how fantastic Daniel looked peeling off a pair of loose black pants and tossing them into the crowd.

One woman caught the pants as they sailed through the air then glared at her friends with undisguised triumph. Almost every woman at the table clutched some article of clothing they'd snagged from the air during the night, but still, they snarled and snipped at the woman holding Daniel's pants as if they were the most coveted souvenir.

Nadia rolled her eyes and focused on the stage just as Daniel's gaze found her. Being her servant, he was immune to her powers and had no trouble seeing her. No doubt he could feel her building irritation as well. Was that the reason for the smirk on his face? Did he think it was funny to watch her scowling at the other women? If so, he was in for it later.

As if reading her thoughts, the smirk turned to a full grin, and he began to dance just for her. Nadia shifted against the bar, struggling to keep her powers from faltering while her body reached out and connected with Daniel.

Every time he licked away a bead of sweat above his lip, she tasted it, and every beat of his heart echoed loud and clear in her ears. She'd wanted this connection, but she'd underestimated how strong it would be. She hadn't expected to feel the music pounding through her, but it vibrated with an intensity that only heightened the excitement she could feel building in Daniel.

Her body reacted to every move he made as if she danced for the raucous crowd. She could feel the stage beneath her feet and the hot lights above her head. The catcalls and whistles were not meant for her, and yet her body reacted to each one until her nipples hardened and her sex throbbed. She did not need to drop her gaze to know Daniel was also aroused, but she looked anyway.

A huge erection strained the confines of the g-string in a most unseemly fashion. No wonder the women's shrieks were strong enough to threaten glass. Following the pulse of the music, he rolled his hips while skimming a hand down the center of his torso. He reached the top of the g-string, toyed with the slim band then dragged his hand back up.

Nadia bit her tongue and reached back to dig her nails into the edge of the bar. The first two dances had been hot, but this one seemed a hell of a lot more seductive. Maybe it was the song? The other two had been faster and Daniel had actually danced, but this song made him slither and gyrate in a way that showcased every muscle running under his sweat-slicked skin. She didn't know how much more she could take.

"Thirsty, love?" The unexpected question tore Nadia's gaze from the stage.

She whipped around to eye the hovering bartender. Like all the guys who worked the club while not on stage, he wore nothing but a pair of small, black shorts. However, the smile he flashed was lovely enough to distract from the body, and that was saying a lot.

"Excuse me?"

"Can I get you a drink? You look thirsty." He winked and nodded toward the stage. "Danny has that effect on lots of women."

Oh God, this conversation could only mean one thing. Her powers were no longer working. If this handsome, flirtatious devil could see her, others could as well. Oops. "No, I'm fine, thank you." Unless he planned to open a vein, there was nothing he could give her to relieve the way she felt.

"Suit yourself," he said with a sexy shrug. "Just give a holler if you change your mind." He turned to head for the other end of the bar but hesitated and looked back. "Oh, you'd be able to see better if you moved closer to the stage, then maybe Danny boy will choose you to enjoy the little bonus at the end of this set." He winked again. "Just a thought."

Bonus? She did not like the sound of that.

Nadia focused on the stage again to see Daniel stretched out on his stomach. The lights played over the shiny muscles of his back, not to mention the way they highlighted the perfection of his ass. He arched off the floor in a yoga-style move before flattening again into a push-up position. He held himself thus for several moments while his gaze scanned the agitated crowd. A smile played at his lips, making him seem dangerously boyish.

With a flick of his head to clear the hair off his forehead, he sprang to his feet in one agile move and turned his back on the audience. The g-string was all but invisible from behind, giving the mouth watering impression that he was naked.

Dear God, maybe she did need a drink. At least alcohol would burn enough to keep her mind focused. But before she could summon the bartender, Daniel tossed a look over his shoulder and hooked his fingers into the waist of his g-string. Smirking, he pulled one side down.

The club erupted into a frenzy of feminine voices shrieking for him to "take it all off." One woman from the annoying table launched herself out of her chair to throw her upper body onto the stage. She reached for Daniel and managed to wrap her fingers around his ankle, but he shook her off, never once faltering in his performance. The woman looked as if she might cry as he tugged the other side of his g-string down. The flimsy fabric hung on to the swell of his penis for dear life, exposing a great deal of tawny pubic hair.

"You look ready to murder someone, love."

Nadia glared at the bartender, hissed and headed toward the stage. Enough was enough, for God's sake.

Chapter Eleven

Daniel tried not to react as Nadia stalked toward the stage, but it was almost impossible not to. The closer she got, the faster his heart pounded. Had he been trying to provoke her by teasing the women to such a degree? Hell yeah.

Seeing her standing at the bar glaring at everyone and barely holding onto her control had awakened the devil in him. He'd wanted to shake her up a bit, and if the look in her eyes was any indication, he'd succeeded.

She stopped at the edge of the stage and fixed him with a piercing, silver stare. He knew that look all too well, and his veins pulsed with the need to give her what she craved.

"What the hell are you doing?" She shot the question at him as if they were the only two able to hear it. At the sound of her voice, the screams faded and the club grew eerily quiet, making the song seem loud and obnoxious as it continued to play.

"Hey!" a woman yelled. "Let him keep going."

"Yeah," said another. "Get out of the way. Who do you think you are?"

Nadia never even flinched. She arched a brow and crossed her arms. "Well? Answer me. What do you think you're doing?"

Daniel snapped his g-string back over his hips and joined Nadia at the edge of the stage. "I'm doing what I get paid to do." Squatting down, he met her angry gaze. "Weren't you enjoying the show?" The fact that she licked her lips and ran her eyes over him was answer enough. She wanted him so bad, he could taste it.

"You said you didn't do naked." Her voice was low, husky and full of hunger. It shot straight to his groin, making him harder than the g-string would allow for. Good thing he was squatting.

"I wasn't going to take it off, Nadia. I was just teasing them." Her eyes darkened, and she reached out to take hold of his wrist.

"Were you teasing them or me?"

"Does it matter?"

Her grip tightened, and she pulled him toward her, hard enough to drop him to his knees. "Answer me."

"It's against the rules to touch," he told her. Her look turned dangerous, shooting a thrill of anticipation through him. It was wrong to egg her on, especially here, but she was so damn sexy when her eyes blazed with hunger.

Still pulling on him, she forced him closer, until he was on his hands and knees and staring straight into her eyes. "So it's probably against the rules to fuck you, too." Her words carried, and the crowd gasped as one.

Daniel laughed. "Yes, that is most definitely against the rules." He was almost positive she wouldn't dare but equally sure he wouldn't stop her if she tried.

Something shifted in her eyes while the edge of her lips curled to reveal her fangs. "You know I don't do well with rules, my darling."

"Nadia." He murmured the amused warning while she leapt onto the stage with one agile move. She gave him no time to register what was happening before she hooked her foot under his arm and sent him sprawling onto his back. Smiling, she planted her spike heel in the center of his chest. If she cared how any of this looked, it didn't show in her steely expression.

"Nadia?" Not even the sound of his voice penetrated the glaze of hunger in her eyes. Scraping the hell out of his chest, he managed to slide out from under her shoe.

She blinked and simply straddled his torso. "Are you trying to get away from me?"

Daniel propped his weight on his hands, intending to move, but froze at the odd tone of Nadia's voice. "No. I'm yours to command, mistress."

Her eyes flashed, and she hunkered down to look directly in his face. The position hiked her skirt high on her thighs, flashing the mouth watering sight of her naked pussy.

Shit, if he got any harder, the damn g-string

would tear.

"I think it was a very bad idea for me to accompany you to work."

Daniel almost laughed. "W-why do you say that?"

Instead of answering, she stroked her nails up the side of his neck and licked her lips. His body caught fire, and he didn't care where they were or the amount of hell there'd be to pay. He wanted her. Palpable hunger radiated off her to mix with lust coursing through him, making him wish he possessed the fangs to take her the way she was about to take him.

"Sorry, gorgeous." Raphael, the co-owner of the place, appeared behind Nadia and reached for her shoulders. Before he could touch her, she whipped around, snapping like a wild animal. He jerked his hand back, barely saving his fingers from her teeth. "Whoa there."

Daniel caught Raphael's questioning gaze and mouthed the words "back off." Thankfully Raphael obeyed, though he looked far from pleased, and Daniel knew it was only a matter of time before Valentino showed up and the shit would surely hit the fan then.

Whether Nadia decided to feed from him or fuck him or whatever her intentions were, he'd be lucky if the worst Valentino did was fire him.

****

Daniel's thoughts and concerns were loud and clear in Nadia's mind, but none of it mattered. She had to have him. Now. Bloodlust roared through her veins like a train unwilling to stop for anything, and ignoring the need would only make it worse. She'd rather infuriate Valentino and cost Daniel his job than go anywhere near any of the other blood pounding through the club.

Kneeling astride him, she pressed her hands to his chest and lowered her face to his. "Do you have any idea how much I need you right now?"

"I think so." He kept his voice low. "I feel it."

Nadia nodded. "Yes, just as I felt every move you made on this stage. I knew the moment your body hardened in response to the crowd's excitement. I tasted the sweat on your lips." She dropped her gaze to his mouth. "I cannot promise to be gentle."

"I don't need gentle." Eagerness seeped into his tone, dragging her attention back to his eyes. "I don't want you to be gentle."

"Oh God, Daniel, what did I do to deserve you?" She kissed him before he could speak and tasting him only made the craving worse. It wasn't enough to have his tongue trapped between her fangs and the rhythm of his heart pounding under her palms, not when the heat of his body penetrated her thighs and maddened her.

Despite the hundreds of watchful eyes, she continued to kiss him while reaching down to hook her fingers in the band of the g-string. His erection already strained the mesh to the point of bursting, and it was nothing to rip the fabric away from his body. He gasped into her mouth as his cock sprang free to rest along his hip. Wasting no time, Nadia curled her fingers around the length and began to stroke.

Daniel ripped his mouth free and arched under her. "Oh God..."

Tossing his head back, he exposed his neck, and Nadia buried her face against the stretched tendons. She licked and nipped at them while her hand continued to coax harsh gasps of pleasure.

The song had ended, and the club lay under a blanket of heavy silence. Daniel's heart raced in Nadia's ears, providing the perfect soundtrack as far as she was concerned. Losing herself in the familiar beat, she pierced his neck and swallowed the first rush of blood. His cock twitched in her hand as he moaned with pleasure.

Control slowly came back to her with every new swallow, and she gathered enough focus to harness the power she needed to immobilize everyone in the club. She'd have to clear their memories later, but for now, it was important to keep them in their seats and away from her and Daniel. No telling what she'd do if anyone tried to interfere.

Confident she had everything under control, Nadia sipped happily at Daniel's neck and shifted to place his cock at the entrance of her wet, needy pussy. He filled her with one thrust and set a nice, easy tempo, which she was able to mimic without compromising her bite on his neck. More proof, not that she required any, that he was the perfect servant.

At some point, Nadia relaxed enough to allow Daniel to gain the upper hand. Without hesitation, he rolled her to her back, forcing her to lose her hold on his neck. She'd had enough to soothe the bloodlust and was more than happy to focus on the other need burning through her. So she did not utter a single protest as he propped his weight on his hands and pushed into her hard enough to slide her along the slick stage. Grabbing his arms, she held on while he rammed into her again.

"I'm going to get fired, you know?"

Nadia smiled at Daniel's ability to think, converse and fuck at the same time. "Tell Valentino I gave you no choice."

He bucked against her hard. "Does it really look like I'm being forced?"

She slid her hand up his arm to cup his cheek. "Stop worrying. No one will remember this." Reaching higher, she brushed his hair out of his eyes. "Unless they are as stubborn as you and choose to remember."

"Will you ever get over that?" He frowned as she took the time to consider her reply.

"Maybe, but I did not enjoy learning that my powers are faulty."

"Only where I'm concerned." With a little growl, he buried his face in the crook of her shoulder. "Enough talking." He grazed her skin with his teeth, mimicking her own actions at his neck, but if he wanted her blood he'd have to ask for it.

"Feed me, mistress."

Ah, the sweetest words imaginable.

Nadia ripped into her wrist, letting the smell of her blood pull Daniel's face away from her neck. Taking all of his weight onto one hand, he managed to maintain the rhythm of his thrusts while locking his mouth around her wound. As always, the sounds and sight of him feeding enflamed her, and her body succumbed to a powerful orgasm. Rolling her head to avoid the sexy sight of Daniel's lips on her wrist, she focused on the crowd.

Several women were having a very hard time remaining immune as they gawked at the stage. They squirmed in their seats and gripped the edge of the table, sure signs that they very much wanted to relieve some naughty ache. Nadia was tempted to tell them to go for it, but good Lord, Val would hang her if she incited a group orgy. Oh, but how much fun would that be? The look on his face would be priceless.

Closing her eyes, she tossed her head back and laughed. She never thought she'd love life again, but she did. With Daniel happily sucking at her wrist while his glorious body throbbed inside her, she was truly happy.

So take that, Master.

Ah, if only she could rub her triumph in his face—

"So go ahead."

Nadia's eyes snapped open, and the blood she'd taken from Daniel froze in her veins.

Chapter Twelve

Daniel went still and met her gaze, but she shook her head to stop the question she could see in his eyes. Fixing her gaze over his shoulder, she blinked several times, but the man standing there did not fade. He was real and he was here.

"Nadia?" When she remained silent, Daniel tossed a look over his shoulder. "Um, why do I have a bad feeling about him?"

Nadia pushed at his shoulders. "Move," she bit out. "Let me up."

Looking less than pleased, he swung his gaze back to her face and stayed right where he was, buried to the hilt inside her. His stubbornness she could do without at the moment.

"Daniel, please."

"You and I need to get a few things straight, mistress."

She nodded, still pushing at his shoulders. "Yes, okay, but not right now. Please." Her master was not known to have unlimited patience, and he wouldn't be here if it weren't important. Right? Wondering what on earth he might want distracted her from Daniel's resistance.

"Who is he?" Daniel's voice brought her back into focus, and she renewed her efforts to push him off.

"Someone I do not want to keep waiting." It was easy to see how unsatisfying her reply was. "Daniel, I swear to you I'll explain everything, but right now you have to let me up."

He laid his mouth against hers but did not kiss her. "I'm not sure I like the look of him or the way you're reacting. If you aren't going to be honest with me, a relationship won't work."

Nadia's stomach twisted. Digging her fingers into his shoulders, she forced him to look at her. "Whatever you do, don't tell me to release you from our bond." God, was she begging?

"Would you, if I did?"

Oh God, she couldn't do this. Not right now. Not with the master looming over them. Tears threatened as desperation took hold of her. "Let me up, I beg you." She dropped her voice and pleaded with her eyes. "Before he forces you to."

To her relief, Daniel pulled out and rolled off her, but not without a good amount of cursing.

"Good decision, boy." Maybe if the master hadn't spoken, or maybe if he'd said anything but that, Daniel would have continued to cooperate. Instead, he jumped to his feet with the clear intent to confront their unwelcome visitor. He didn't take more than one step, however, before the tingling of her master's power became unmistakable.

Damn, she hadn't wanted him to control Daniel. His gaze found her, and she flinched under the cold weight of it. Oh God, whatever the reason for this visit, it was probably very bad.

The master held out his hand. "Come with me, and I'll release your young man."

Nadia climbed to her feet and smoothed her dress down. Anxiety filled her as she glanced at Daniel. "Please don't hurt him." Something odd filled the master's eyes, but she couldn't name the emotion. It was telling enough that he'd allowed anything to show.

"When I discovered you were not where Fabian had been ordered to take you, I thought it would be a good idea to find you. Foolishly, I feared you might be in danger." His cold gaze slid to Daniel and then swept out over the club. "My fears were unfounded it seems."

Nadia swallowed and tasted shame. There had to be something she could say to explain all of this, but before she could come up with anything logical, the master shook his head and took hold of her arm. His touch burned with the power he used to control, not only Daniel, but the rest of the club as well, and she gasped at the shock.

"We'll talk in private, because unlike yourself, I do not care for an audience."

Oh dear, she knew that cold, controlled tone.

With a look toward Daniel, she had no choice but to allow her master to guide her toward the back of the stage. In their wake, the club erupted into a frenzy of confusion. Nadia glanced back, but the master merely tugged her forward, forcing her to watch where she was going or fall flat on her face.

"No one will recall what they witnessed."

Nadia glanced at his profile, seeing all the signs of barely restrained anger in his features. What right did he have to be angry? She was the one being dragged off like an errant child. "I don't care if they do or not."

Stopping, he turned to face her, still keeping a firm grip on her wrist. "Have I taught you nothing? Does it mean nothing to you, the danger you bring upon our kind with such a display?"

"As if anything I do can affect you and yours anymore." Surprisingly, she was able to yank her arm free. For reasons she did not wish to investigate, his touch bothered her. "I no longer have any association with the coven, so why do you care what I do?"

"You are still a vampire, Nadia, and you still answer to me." Taking hold of her again, he pulled her further down the narrow hall until they reached Valentino's office. Oh, marvelous, as if this was where she wished to be.

Valentino stood as they entered, his face reflecting mild surprise. "What the...?" His gaze found the master. "What are you doing here?"

Anger and a hint of anxiety tightened his voice.

"At ease, Valentino, my visit has nothing to do with you." The master pushed Nadia into the closest chair. "Do you have any idea what was going on out there?"

Valentino glared at Nadia. "What did she do?"

"She was in the process of giving your audience quite the education in vampire/servant relations."

"I told Daniel you were not welcome here, and yet here you are. Does he mean that little to you that you would risk his job? Or didn't he tell you that I'd fire him?

"He told me about your threats, yes. I had no intention of being seen this evening."

"Which lasted how long?" the master asked.

Nadia glanced up and over her shoulder. "Why are you here?"

"Answer my question, Nadia. How long did you manage to remain undetected?"

"I was doing just fine until Daniel started his third set."

"And tell me," the master paused, leaning down to grip the arms of the chair so his eyes were level with hers. "What exactly happened during that third set to provoke you to have sex on stage?"

"Oh, my God." Valentino dropped into his chair and continued to curse under his breath. "Tell me you didn't."

Nadia ignored him, keeping her gaze fixed

on her master. "I got jealous."

"A dangerous curse for you, it seems. I would have thought you'd learn from past mistakes."

"Exiling me can't change who I am, and I do not enjoy watching unworthy women attempt to steal the affection of the men I—" she stopped before the word could slip out.

"You do not love me, Nadia." He straightened and shook his head at her. "I have always suspected it was the idea of me you loved. Or perhaps the status it would give you."

"How dare you!" Nadia jumped out of the chair. "I have no idea why I wasted a single moment feeling anything for you."

Without a flicker of emotion, the master slid his attention past her shoulder. "Would you give us some privacy, Valentino?"

"Gladly." With a dark look in her direction, Valentino left the office.

Nadia attacked the moment the door closed. "Why would you believe what I feel is not real? You saved me..." Her voice cracked, but she refused to back down. "How could I not love you for that?"

"It was my duty to save you, Nadia. How could I leave you alone and unprotected?"

"Your duty? I was nothing more than a duty?" She felt ill. She'd never meant a thing to him. While she craved to love him, he viewed her as he did all the other coven members, as a responsibility. Nothing more.

"You are not like all the others, Nadia."

Nadia slumped back into the chair and crossed her arms. "If you read my mind, I refuse to have this conversation with you."

"Fine, we'll do this your way." A few moments of silence ticked by until he finally sighed. "What possessed you to behave in such a fashion? What I witnessed seemed to stem from more than mere jealousy."

"Exactly how much did you see?"

His lips twitched. "Enough. You were a woman possessed, Nadia, and I always believed you had more control over your emotions than that."

She shrugged, wondering why it really mattered. "Yes, well, Daniel happens to taste better than anyone I've ever had. I was hungry, he was there, I wanted him..." Another shrug. "What is there to explain?"

"I see." Those annoying words were followed by a long, searching stare.

Nadia shifted, growing more and more uncomfortable with each passing second, until she couldn't take it anymore. "What?" she nearly barked. "Just say whatever it is you are thinking."

"What would you say if I told you I'd come here to offer you a second chance?"

Everything inside Nadia tightened. "A second chance at what?"

"A second chance at everything. If I told you, you could return to the coven, what would you do?"

Very slowly, she stood up. "Is that what you're saying? Is that why you are here?" Maybe he did care. "Does your queen know about this?"

"Do you believe she does not?"

Okay, now she was confused. "Are you really saying I can return?"

"Yes, under one condition."

"Yes, yes, I must swear fealty to the queen—"

"No," he interrupted. "You may come back if you leave your young man behind."

Thank God the chair was still right behind her, because she did not relish the thought of falling on the floor as her knees buckled. "What? Why would I do that? My servants are lost to me, are they not? I felt the bond break, which was horrible, I might add. How can you expect me to return without Daniel? And why would you make me?"

"Yes, Jason and Chase are both bound to others."

"And Lukas?"

Something shifted on the master's face. "Lukas was asked to leave, and that is all I will say on the matter."

And she knew better than to push. Lukas had always been a self-serving loose cannon, that he'd done something to get on the master's last nerve did not surprise her in the least. But none of that mattered. What mattered was why on earth she could go back only if she left Daniel here. It was a ludicrous choice to have to make, and she said as much.

The master merely shrugged. "So then the answer is no. Very well."

"Wait a damn minute." Nadia stood, but before she could say more, the door opened and the object of their conversation stalked in.

Daniel had pulled the black pants on, and briefly she wondered if he'd had to wrestle them from the audience member. Aside from the pants, he was bare-chested, barefoot and covered in sweat. His hair was scraped back from his face, revealing the hostile look in his eyes. The master, elegantly casual in black pants and a black sweater, made Daniel seem wild and savage, and Nadia was startled that such a boyishly handsome face could project such rage.

"So, you are the bastard who kicked her out?"

The master smiled and flicked his gaze toward Nadia. Doing so left him vulnerable, and Daniel's punch took him completely off guard. The hit packed enough gusto to nearly send the master crashing to the floor.

"Daniel!" Nadia was at his side in an instant, clutching his tense arm. "For heaven's sake, don't do that again."

The master recovered quickly and fingered the blood leaking from his split lip. He actually smiled at Daniel. "Yes, I am the bastard who exiled her."

Daniel growled and took a step closer, but Nadia maintained her hold on his arm. "Stop it," she hissed. "He's here to tell me I can go back." Her words earned her Daniel's full attention.

"Oh yeah? What's the catch?"

The master laughed and thumped Daniel on the shoulder, which earned him a rather irritated glance. "You're a smart lad. The catch is she cannot take you along."

"And she told you to go to hell, right?" The master shrugged, and Daniel turned to Nadia. "Right?" When she didn't answer right away, his gaze narrowed. "Nadia, answer me. You cannot go back, or at least without me. What about the bond that's between us and all the stuff you told me about how unbreakable it is—"

"Did she not mention the servants she had to leave behind? There were three of them, and I assure you, leaving one will be easier."

Nadia glared at her master. "Do not make this worse."

Appearing not the least bit apologetic, the master looked from her to Daniel. "Would you two like a moment of privacy?"

"As if you can't hear through the door," Nadia mumbled.

"Regardless, I'll wait outside." Before leaving, he thumped Daniel on the shoulder once more. "She said she felt the bond she shared with the others breaking. Were you there for that?"

Daniel seemed unsure, so Nadia answered

for him. "Yes."

Daniel shot her a questioning look. "When?"

"The night I came here. The night I made you mine. Your blood and your body took the pain of that loss away, but it was not my intent to bind you to me." The master slipped out while Daniel stared at her.

"Will leaving me cause you that much pain?"

"Do you plan on seeking out another vampire mistress?"

"No." He sounded and looked disgusted by the suggestion. "I can't even figure out the one I have."

Nadia shrugged and lowered her gaze. "Then no, I should be fine."

At least she would be once the sick feeling in her stomach subsided. She'd been angry and hurt when leaving Jason and Chase behind, but the thought of leaving Daniel...well, what she felt was so much more.

Making her way back to the chair, she took a much needed seat.

"Are you all right?" Daniel crossed the room to kneel at her feet. "You don't look so good."

"Gee, thanks." Nadia chuckled at the crestfallen look on Daniel's face. "I'm kidding, but no, I don't think I'm all right."

Cautiously, he rested his hands on her knees. "Isn't this what you want, the chance to go back? You told me how restless you feel, how afraid you are of becoming bored. Maybe you should go back among your own kind—"

"Daniel—"

"No," he shook his head. "If he's giving you the chance to have everything you want, then I won't stand in your way. What we had, or what we might have had, was great, but I'll understand if it's not enough for you."

The sick feeling intensified, making her remember what it felt like to be very mortal and capable of vomiting. It wasn't a memory she appreciated. But she also didn't appreciate Daniel's willingness to let her go. What was that all about? Shouldn't he be begging her to stay? Shouldn't he tell her how much he loves her and needs her? Didn't he know how much she loved and needed him? Oh God, she'd never told him.

She dropped her face into her hands, unable to bear the look in Daniel's hazel eyes, but he wouldn't let her hide for long. Taking hold of her wrists, he lowered her hands and forced her to meet his gaze.

"If you're going to go, at least look me in the eye while you tell me good-bye."

"Do you really love me?" He'd said as much, but they were words anyone could say. Jason and Chase had professed their love for her, and Chase had even cried at the thought of her leaving, and yet Daniel's eyes were bone dry. If he really loved her, could he watch her walk away without shedding a tear?

"Nadia, I'm only twenty-three, do I really have any idea what love is?"

"Yes, I think you do, and I need to know if

you really love me because I'm very afraid that I might actually love you." There, she'd said it, and the world had not ended.

Daniel stood and used the grip he had on her wrists to pull her to her feet. "Tell me why it scares you?"

For God's sake, did he have to start asking questions? Couldn't he just profess his undying love, beg her to stay and end this miserably uncomfortable moment of self discovery? The look in his eyes said, no, he wasn't going to do any of that without some answers first.

Nadia sighed. "It scares me because for the last hundred years or so I believed I was in love."

"With the guy in the hall?"

"The guy in the hall happens to be my master and the leader of a very large coven."

Daniel didn't seem too impressed. "So? He still bleeds when you hit him, or didn't you notice?"

Nadia managed a smile. "Oh yes, I noticed, and that was very stupid."

"Blame it on hot-headed youth. Now answer me. Is he the one you thought you loved?"

"Yes."

"And the servants he mentioned? You had three?" There was a bit of shock in that last question.

"Yes, I had three." She tried to read his expression as he mulled over her response, but his eyes were unusually blank. "Why do I feel the need to apologize for even having one servant before you?" His expression softened, and he pulled her into one of the tight hugs she had grown to adore.

"You don't have to apologize for anything you did before coming here. Just tell me that one is enough from now on?"

Nadia nodded with her face buried against Daniel's sweaty chest. Unable to help herself, she licked a bead of moisture away, savoring the salty taste.

"Does this mean you're going to refuse his offer to go back? Because you should stop licking me if you're still thinking about leaving me."

She licked him again and shifted to nip at his nipple. His arms tightened around her then he reached up to bury his hands deep in her hair, pulling her head back until their eyes met.

After studying her face for a few moments, he smiled. "Uh oh, you have that look."

"What look?" But she knew. Hunger burned in her veins, lust heightened her senses and the overwhelming need to have Daniel every way possible made her eyes water and her throat dry.

"You know exactly what look, you vixen." All of a sudden his expression sobered. "Am I crazy for agreeing to this vampire/servant deal? You have yet to tell me what's in it for me, you know?"

Nadia harrumphed. "You mean besides the honor of serving me?"

"Yeah, besides that." Despite the subtle grin, Daniel's tone was still serious.

"The benefits, if you choose to call them that, change depending on how much of my blood you consume. As it stands now, your awareness of me should be incredibly fine tuned, and if you focused all your efforts, you may be able to hear my thoughts."

"Hmm, interesting. I'll have to see if that works later." He winked. "But I take it I will still age and eventually die?"

If Nadia hadn't been wrapped tightly in Daniel's embrace, the question might have brought her to her knees. His death was not something she wished to contemplate, and preventing it from ever happening was high on her list. If he agreed.

Swallowing the lump in her throat, she searched for the right words to say. "As I said, the more blood you take, the more benefits there are." He looked ready to probe deeper, but she cupped her hand over his mouth and shook her head. "No, we'll talk more about that later. If you want me to stay, and you know that means I'll be staying for a very long time, say so and I'll tell the master to leave and never come back."

"I want you to stay for a very long time." He said it with no hesitation and while staring straight into her eyes. The combination sent a thrill through her like she'd never felt before. While her eyes watered, he leaned down to kiss her. "I think I might end up quitting the club after all."

Nadia pulled back, surprised by the shift in conversation. "What? Why? Oh...because of tonight? Look, I'm very sorry, and I promise no one will remember a thing come morning—"

It was his turn to lay his hand over her mouth. "Shh. It's not because of that, well, maybe it is a little, but I think I should try and make a go of the Marine Biology thing. I spent a lot of money to get that degree, and well, I can't strip forever."

If she ended up making him a vampire, he could, but she held her tongue. "Does this mean we're going to the Amazon?" She failed to keep the horror from her voice.

Daniel laughed and kissed her again. "You'll like it."

"No, I really do not think I will. It's very hot, and there are wild animals, and I bet it smells." She wrinkled her nose.

"I'll be there, and I don't think clothes are a necessity among the natives." He spoke between kisses and began to back her toward the door.

"Oh, you are a devil." Winding her arms around his neck, she captured his mouth in a long, thorough kiss then pulled back. "I suppose I cannot allow you to run naked through the jungle without supervision."

His expression grew serious. "I love you."

Nadia's eyes burned as she traced the full line of Daniel's lower lip. "Thank you." Maybe she should have said she loved him back, but her quiet words filled his eyes with pure joy.

Pulling her into a tight hug, he buried his face in her hair. "You're very welcome."

Epilogue

Amazon Rainforest—one year later

"Are you sure about this?" Nadia's question was almost lost among the nights sounds. Exotic birds and agitated monkeys squawked high in the trees while a myriad of insects competed in the undergrowth. She hunkered down under a towering tree and watched Daniel peel off his clothes.

"I am very sure, or I would not have asked." He tossed his shirt and shorts into the leaf litter and closed the distance between them. "Now stop doubting me and just do it." Grabbing her hand, he pulled her to her feet.

"I just don't want you to regret this at some point in the future. There is no going back, you know?" He swept her hair off her forehead and flashed the smile that never failed to ignite a fire in her blood.

"I will not regret it anymore than I regret a single moment I've spent with you."

"But what about your work? This will affect everything, Daniel—"

He covered her mouth. "What I do requires twenty-four hours of commitment, and the other workers won't mind handing the night shift off to me."

There were no more arguments for her to make, and to be honest, she was tired of protesting. It thrilled her to know that Daniel wanted this change almost as much as she wanted it. So why was she hesitating?

"The longer you stand there thinking about it, the more convinced I am that you aren't willing to do this."

She quickly shook her head, hating that he doubted her. "No. I just had to be sure." Gently, she pressed against his chest. "I want you comfortable, so lie down."

Without hesitation, he stretched out on the forest floor and propped his hands under his head. "Good?"

Nadia scanned the length of Daniel's naked body and moistened her lips. "Oh yes, very good."

With great care, she removed her clothing, which did not take long. One of the positive things about living in the forest was the ease of not having to wear a great deal. No one seemed to mind when she walked about in nothing but a skimpy dress and sandals, and she certainly enjoyed Daniel's habit of wearing only shorts and flip-flops. When she was as naked as he, she knelt at his side and ran her hand down the center of his torso.

He shivered slightly and settled his gaze on her face. "I do have one question."

"Ask me anything." Nadia kept her focus on the contrast of her pale fingers over Daniel's golden skin.

"After this is done, I won't be your servant."

She shifted her gaze to his face. "No. We'll have to find another means of sustenance." She'd thought long and hard about this very matter, and the conclusion she'd come to shocked her now just as much as it had when it first entered her mind.

"I can tell you've thought about it. Care to tell me what you've come up with?"

"I think it would be best if we evolve." She nearly choked on the last word. Somewhere, Hell was likely freezing over.

Daniel chuckled. "You look so incredibly horrified." He slid a hand free to caress her cheek. "It will not kill you to drink your next meal out of a cup."

"No, but I'm not looking forward to it."

Suddenly, he pushed up onto his elbows, his expression deadly serious. "You do not have to do this. It's not my intention to deprive you of what you enjoy." He reached for her hands. "If you don't think you can survive without my blood, then don't even try."

"Stop it." She snatched her hands away and pushed him back down. "I've made my decision and drinking synthetic blood is a small price to pay to know that you will always be at my side."

"Good." Once more he propped his hands under his head. "Is there anything I need to do?"

Nadia shook her head and shifted to straddle Daniel. "Just relax and trust me not to hurt you."

"A little pain is okay, I thought you knew that?" His eyes danced, and a devilish smirk played at his lips.

"Fine, I won't hurt you too much." Focusing on his neck, she watched the pulse beat at the hollow of his throat. It would be gone this time tomorrow, as would the heat of his skin and the sound of his heart. Never again would she taste the sweet vitality of his blood.

"You're thinking too hard again."

She pulled her gaze from Daniel's neck. "I'll miss your taste."

"So drink your fill now. Tonight." He rolled his head to the side, exposing his jugular. "Bite me, mistress."

Nadia did not have to be told twice. She leaned down, inhaling the musky aroma of Daniel's skin and absorbing the warmth of his body into her palms. Sinking her teeth into his throat, she broke the skin, pierced the artery and sucked hard. The first gush of blood made her moan, and she shifted closer to bite deeper.

Daniel wrapped his arms around her to move her over his cock. He positioned the head at her opening, and while she swallowed another gulp, he pushed inside. Another moan shook Nadia, and she pressed down, taking every inch of him until there was nowhere left for him to go. They moved together, slowly, languidly while his blood enflamed her veins.

When it was time, she slid her teeth free to rip open her wrist. Daniel watched with lazy eyes. He no longer thrust in and out of her, but he was still hard and very present inside the tight sheath of her sex. The moment her blood appeared on her skin, he licked his lips and closed his eyes. Laying her wrist over his mouth, she coaxed him to take the final step.

With the first brush of his tongue, his fate was sealed. Nothing and no one would ever come between them. She would not allow it. She would teach Daniel all he needed to know to survive and be the sort of creator all vampires deserved. He would never find himself abandoned or alone, but most importantly, she would love him and treasure him for what he was, the other half of her soul.

Nadia almost laughed out loud. Wouldn't the master be proud?

A word about the author...

L. Rosario's interest in vampires began when she devoured Anne Rice's Interview with a Vampire. Until she actually gets the opportunity to interview one of her own, she'll content herself with creating steamy stories featuring sexy vampires and oh so willing victims.

Visit L's site at www.lrosario.com
To learn more, visit L's blog at
www.spaces.msn.com/vampdarling